AURORA DAYS

THE BARDO TRILOGY - 1

MALA NAIDOO

Naidoo, Mala

Title: *Aurora Days*

ISBN - 979-0-6484854-5-2 (Paperback)

ISBN – 978-0-6484854–6-9 (ebook)

ABOUT THE AUTHOR

Mala Naidoo is an Australian author. She was born in South Africa during the apartheid era which is the impetus for her fictional stories that take on a life of their own when the creative muse beckons. Mala believes that literature speaks through the values and culture of characters' lives, situations, and choices, instilling understanding through connections to a moment in time, an event or conversation that brings clarity to daily existence. Mala is also a teacher who upholds justice on *All Lives Matter*.

ALSO BY MALA NAIDOO

Across Time and Space

Vindication Across Time

Souls of Her Daughters

Chosen Lives

What Change May Come

The Rain - A Collection of Short Stories (ebook)

Life's Seasons - A Collection of Short Stories

Random Heart Poetry—Light and Shade

*With gratitude to my parents who instilled a restlessness for justice,
equity and democracy*

What's to come is still unsure; in delay, there lies no plenty

~William Shakespeare's Twelfth Night~

V iola glanced at her watch — she dreaded leaving but nothing would stop her, not even Rob Dwyer, headmaster at Blackwater Ridge Performing Arts Academy. Rob was a small part of her anxiety. When Tempest called, she had to answer the instruction to move on. It was a guess when she would be asked to leave to take up a new position — anywhere in the world. Flexibility was core to her other passion. Her teaching contracts for the past three years never included a full year of work, in any one location. Blackwater was home to her, letting her come and go as she did. She owed Rob much.

Her eager students fixed their hurt eyes on her. All were talented musicians having earned scholarships to this prestigious academy. They knew she was not their permanent teacher, but she grew on them like she did each year in a new class of young starry-eyed musicians.

'Can't you stay until the end of the year, Ms Bardo, then leave after we've finished.'

'I can't do that Cassie. I have a limited contract here and have to move to my next position.'

'Why can't someone else leave... like *you-know-who...*'

Tommy Rainer glanced around their small class of twelve students, ranging from thirteen to fifteen years, with a devilish grin. Her talented, beyond their years, students — intense and passionate, were innocent and playful around her. She allowed them to be who they were, and detested molding students, caging their personalities and artistic talents were counterproductive to creativity. She knew that creativity came with a sensitivity that few understood — those days of solitude — moodiness and then sheer delight, flitting between emotions that others labeled and mocked. Her students' emotional reactions were natural responses as teenagers but intensified with their artistic passion. Experience had taught her that soon they would clash with societal and familial expectations.

It was almost 10:45 am, Rob Dwyer would be ready, to convince her to change her decision. He always welcomed her like the prodigal daughter when she asked to return to Blackwater Performing Arts Academy. Staff had tested his goodwill in recent months and Viola gave him her commitment and integrity which garnered negative attention as Rob's special one — her frequent flights away from Blackwater and sudden returns annoyed those who saw it as a privilege. He was reclusive avoiding confrontation with disgruntled staff. Going to Rob's office might be viewed by some as seeking favors. Someone was always watching her movements, or perhaps his.

When she was thirty-nine she learned to accept that she could never change some things. She had a purpose, a life calling that took her on two journeys each year and that was all that mattered in her life now.

'Good morning, Mr Dwyer, how are you? Thank you for seeing me.'

'Viola, when are you going to stop being so formal. You are the only teacher on staff who calls me Mr Dwyer.'

'I prefer the formal address to keep students doing the same. Too often I hear the lack of formality from a few disrespectful students.'

'My role-model teacher! You come and go, and I wish you would stay on as permanent staff. Can I pressure you to stay on until year end? I will extend your contract today. Say the word for a new contract in this minute. Well, I have one in my desk drawer, hoping...' His pleading eyes made him a desperate schoolboy not her headmaster.

She stared out the window at the music center at the end of the oval, a haven for a passionate music teacher. It was perfect and yet it was not to be her permanent work abode. She had the itch and her heart spoke on where she should be during her time away.

'I'm so sorry to do this to you, but it's not possible this time. I leave for Greece in three days.'

'Is there a remote chance that this is to be your last time away from us? Don't you want to put roots down, leave your mark in one place....' Consternation hardened her eye, and deepened the crevice on her nose bridge with thoughts on how dare he say this, who is he to tell her to settle, did he even know enough about her? She stopped. Rob had been generous to her, he was thinking of the school, not her, and she had to stick to her decision. There was no way out of what she had to do because she chose this life and would not turn her back on that decision. For the past three years she came and went for a term or two and as much as Rob couldn't see it, this was her home base school. Australian shores drew her back each time whether it was because there was a hiatus from her calling with Tempest or an assignment needed her attention on home soil. Home was her compass of return.

Viola's dual life took her to death's door a few times and had her questioning whether she was on the wrong side of the law. Moral law. A petite stature, much like her mother, belied the iron strength she carried. Her mother worked at a university in South Africa after leaving Australia, and her father moved back to his ancestral home in Portugal. With a father as a prolific artist and her mother a professor of literature, it was no surprise that the creative arts fascinated her. She crafted her book of poems under the pseudonym Artista B, but fear kept her from having them published. As a child her father called her his Artista and soon she was Artista to both parents and their close family and friends. Not that there were many in the solitary work lives of her parents.

Viola's air ticket was purchased from her separate savings account for her overseas trips. Her bags were packed and the school in Greece was expecting her as their Australian exchange teacher.

Rob persisted, 'Why Greece, any special reason?'

'Some of my paternal ancestry is Greek although my father is Portuguese.'

This silenced him. How could he argue about planting her feet here when she was going back to some part of her roots for a time? That she would return was what he accepted of all her departures.

Rob saw the honest sparkling delight in her eyes. Would she return was his concern, but he dared not pose that to her now?

'Stay in touch, Viola, I look forward to having you back — any idea how long you plan to be away?'

'I can't say just yet.' She stood up to shake his hand, 'Thank you for everything. I will be in touch, I promise.'

She heard his whispered words, 'Every time you leave it's like sending my child off into the unknown.' He hung onto her hand for an extra second. Viola had to let the guilt wash over her, Rob was going through difficult times. His leadership was under attack from some Iago personalities on staff.

Tempest arranged the exchange position at the Aurora Arts

Academy in Athens. A level of trepidation filled her in knowing she would step onto the corridors of a part of her unknown ancestry. She felt like an impostor, and guilty for using this card to stop Rob. She had to prepare herself for whatever her mission was in Greece. All she was taking was a large backpack as carry-on luggage which included two pairs of jeans, four shirts, two white and two black, three cotton dresses and one black evening dress. She had to travel light or expect to leave excess baggage at each post. The money she earned from teaching in Australia, she saved for her return. On the road she lived a menial existence, ate, and dressed simply, and avoided getting close to people she might not want to see again. Anonymity earned her an unfair reputation of being haughty, and perhaps struggling with some anxiety disorder. She had to let it go, personal sensitivities were counterproductive to her line of work. If there's one thing she learned from being in Tempest's department, it was to toughen up. Her father believed if one could not shape up to the demands of life then they should ship out and save themselves the disgrace of being perceived incompetent. She had a journal, and her iPad packed in her larger than usual handbag, hoping she would not get pulled up at the departure checkpoint for having over one piece of carry-on luggage.

As an only child she was a loner by nature and kept her private counsel with fierce diligence. This made her an ideal candidate to slip in and out of Tempest's requests. A no pay-check job to improve the lot of some and reinstate justice wherever she could, was enough to rest her weary head when she was out on a mission. She had to conduct more research on the school and chose not to call her father for hands-on information about the place. Her mother who knew about that side of her father's roots would want to know more about her mission, would caution her, and tell her father to call her to probe into why she was really going to Greece — too much prying irked her. All she knew was that accommodation was available at the school for overseas teachers and that the headmaster would meet her at the airport when she arrived in Athens. She was not expecting five-star treatment although the private school attracted one of the country's highest fees with its elite parent clientele. The only concern she had, was that the school was a little out of the CBD — she didn't drive and wondered whether this would be a deterrent to the after-hours work Tempest had lined up for her. The school population, she discovered on their website, comprised students whose parents were overseas delegates living and working on international government policies in Greece.

ONCE IN HER WINDOW SEAT, she curled into a ball thankful for passing through the check-in with ease, and that nobody sat next to her. It was not a full flight much to her delight. She paged through the Athenian school brochure and studied the face of the headmaster in this elite Academy. His Vulcan shaped head and narrow eyes made her shiver. It was too early to form judgements, something she knew early in this moon-lighting role. Forming speculations too soon had a way of pointing her in the wrong direction. His expression was hard to read. Rob was an open book. The whole school knew his moods. He locked himself behind his large office door but Aurora's Arts Academy headmaster appeared as cold as alabaster on the shiny pages of this expensive school brochure. He was meeting her at the airport which would allow her time to observe his behavior.

She scrutinized the photograph, the assistant head standing next to him was a younger man, rather diminutive and insignif-icant in the towering height of the headmaster. He appeared to be a last-minute penciled-in inclusion in the photograph. Inter-esting, perhaps he was a yes man. She disliked those sorts —

spineless, complaining and accepting of everything dished down to them. It excited her to be working in a school that had an outstanding reputation for being the best in the country. She dozed off dreaming about sun-soaked beaches and her father painting the landscape before them. He wanted her to spend Christmas with him, she considered taking him up on the offer by deferring her return to Australia. Her Australian Christmases were lonely. She cooked a lean turkey drumstick for one with a single serve of steamed frozen veggies and enjoyed a small cup-cake size Woollies Christmas cake dressed in thick layer of marzipan. Her sweet tooth was a known weakness.

With no inkling into what Tempest had in store for her, she had to wait for instructions before she made Christmas plans. She knew her mother had dregs of extended family living somewhere in Greece but avoided asking questions about them. One conversation with her mother when she was thirteen stuck with her. She asked if she missed the culture and people of her birth country. Her reply was, 'Viola you are an African-French-Portuguese so anywhere in the world is home to you. Resilience is vital to survive in a world of vast opportunity.' She would never get a straight answer, always it was a life lesson like a textual literary evaluation that her mother felt compelled to explain. At thirteen years old those words shaped the direction she took. This was her first trip to Greece where some hidden part of her cultural origins lay. She had no intention of searching for them. Australia was home.

She leaned over to her large handbag for her iPad when she felt a pair of eyes drilling through her from across the aisle — the old woman did the staring, the young man next to her, perhaps in his late teens or early twenties was asleep. When Viola locked eyes with the starer, she averted her eyes to the television screen. It was perhaps an idle stare, long haul flights made people curious about lone travelers. This heightened sense of observation she imbibed from her father. His precision and attention to detail in his paintings made him an acclaimed artist in Africa and Portugal. He ran his own gallery and hosted artists' in-residence workshops at his centre for eclectic art in Porto. She missed him the most when he was teaching, and inventing wonderful works with no break for months at a time.

She looked across at the woman again. Her curly mop of ash-gray hair made her look older than her unwrinkled face. Her deep-set eyes in those fleeting seconds of observation held no expression — a blank, cold stare. The woman fascinated her enough to pull out her journal from the bottom of her bag. Poetry was her release from tension and baking relaxed her. Now she had no oven and a level of tension coupled with curiosity drew her to pen and paper.

> *Stranger with eyes so deep*
> *Sullen without sleep...*

SHE WROTE, drew a line across her words, started anew and soon gave up. Sleep beckoned and she needed to be fresh and alert when she met her new employer and his sidekick. She coiled herself in the cuddly blanket, reached out for another on the vacant seat beside her and stared into space willing a few hours of sleep.

2

—————————

I t was Memorial Day.

THE HEAD of the school and his assistant met her upon arrival
as a courtesy settling in policy for overseas teachers. Trepidation crept in, regardless of the number of places she visited.
Would they like her, think she was a good fit for the school, or
would they treat her with indifference as a foreigner? Her
credentials and experience spoke of her excellence. But worry
she did. She did it well. This is when she needed to crunch on
some peanut brittle — her soother for her soul, a quick sugar
fix. Anxiety gripped. Her jaw tensed and her mouth was dry.
Schools had a way of making Viola feel like a student on her
first day at a new school. She would be spending most of her
days at Aurora Arts Academy and some nights outside
depending on Tempest's agenda.

Miles Alexakis and Jace Dimakos welcomed her, one with a
broad smile, the other with a nod and faint smile. Miles Alexakis introduced himself as the headmaster of the Academy and

Jace as his assistant. They were as the school brochure presented, the tall head and the hesitant assistant, penciled in the shadow behind the looming headmaster.

Miles' booming voice jolted Viola back to reality, 'Welcome, Ms Bardo, you must be nervous and excited at the same time. How was your flight? Did they look after you?' Viola paused unsure which question to answer first, she chose to ignore the part about being nervous.

'Great flight thanks, and thank you for meeting me. Yes, I'm excited to be joining your staff.'

Jace, a man closer to her age, she presumed, sidled up to her with a smile that grew warmer.

'Everyone is eager to meet you. Your reputation precedes you. Mr Alexakis highlighted your credentials at the last staff meeting. Some staff members will be at our formal breakfast to welcome you. Because it's a long weekend, some are away with their families.'

Viola cringed that staff had already scrutinized her credentials. Her private self, hated anyone knowing everything about her before she had met them. Strangers probing into her life!

Jace continued the conversation, keen to impress, asking questions she perceived would come.

'Are you Australian by birth or naturalized?'

'I was born in Mozambique, my parents migrated to Australia when I was a child. My father is Mozambiqan Portuguese, my mother is part African, part French, so my heritage is international.' Viola laughed although often the probing into her background annoyed her. She wanted to be herself, not a Portuguese, French, African-Australian. Being Viola Bardo was enough for her. Miles Alexakis nodded, taking it all in, not commenting.

'I would love to hear more about your intriguing heritage in the days ahead.' Jace chirped, smiling at the headmaster for approval as though he had discovered that which needed further investigation. Viola sensed it was best to avoid him, it could become too personal, too close and she would not risk exposing the real reason why she was in Greece.

'Ms Bardo, so do you plan the number of teacher exchange programs you take on. You seem to have worked in a diverse selection of schools.'

'It has been twice a year. My Australian school is my home base and a place that respects and accepts my decision to be a traveling teacher, I suppose. They have asked me to set down roots soon, so I will wait and see.'

Jace jumped in, 'Perhaps this is where you will set down your roots.' Miles' sidelong glance at Jace brought his enthusiasm to an abrupt halt. Viola had to break the awkward moment.

'Well, to quote Theodore Roethke in 'The Waking' — 'I learn by going where I have to go.'

'Ah, a lover of poetry too! A free spirit.' Miles Alexakis' white teeth sparkled in the sunlight. 'They must value you to have you come and go as you please, so we are the fortunate ones then.'

'That's kind of you, Mr Alexakis.'

'I see you use a formal address, we are on formal terms here at Aurora Arts Academy, because we thrive on our values and excellence.'

'It was a different conversation with my headmaster before I left, he cannot get me to call him by his first name, so formality comes naturally to me. My protocol to remind me not to get ahead of myself and to remain respectful.'

'You are already one of us,' Miles laughed, 'title and rank are things we respect. Your experience will be valuable to all schools.'

'I love traveling, teaching and exotic cuisine, so it's a good combination for me.' Viola felt the lightening of her interactions with the two newcomers in her world. She observed that

Jace remained in Miles' shadow, a terrier with a nervous tail. Too placid! As much as she wanted to avoid close associations, she needed a friend when she was on a foreign assignment.

Before Miles jumped into the driver's seat his show of chivalry in opening the back door for Viola was accompanied by a slight bow. She had better not get used to this, for nobody she knew back home would be opening doors for her!

'Not long to go now,' Jace clucked, turning back from the front passenger seat to look at her.

'It's a public holiday, you both should rest and do what you enjoy on your days off.'

'We pride ourselves on our hospitality to our visiting teachers. Don't worry, perfect timing that you arrived during our Memorial Day weekend, we can give you more attention than would have been possible on a school day, you know.'

'Thank you.'

The car stopped at ornate, wrought iron gates with the gigantic heads of two lions enthroned on the towering pillars supporting the gates. The gatehouse attendant walked up to the car to shake Miles' hand before letting them in. Viola was in awe of the tight security and wondered if that was the only entry and exit point. They drove down a long tree lined path to a cluster of red brick cottages, the main school building was to the right of the cottages. A high wall separated the school from the visiting staff residential quarters. Miles pulled up outside cottage number eight and handed Viola a set of keys. He helped her open the door and told her that, Maria, the boarder mistress and hospitality staff, would escort her down to breakfast in the main hall.

'You have your own private cottage with a bathroom, a bedroom and a little study and kitchenette. Your home while you are with us. You may take all your meals in the dining hall or cook your own. Maria will do the orientation on that. Welcome to Aurora Arts Academy, Ms Bardo. I'll see you at breakfast in an hour.' Miles did a mini bow and stepped backwards off the tiny verandah and Jace did a two-hands wriggling fingers wave.

Viola surveyed the deserted school grounds from behind the wall in front of her cottage. The residential quarters were isolated from the rest of the buildings. The cottages looked new perhaps built in the last three years. She took a quick peek at her phone before a shower. A message from Tempest arrived when she landed. Every time Viola was on an exchange assignment there was a strong psychic connection between them down to the minute.

Hope you had a pleasant flight and are settling in by the time you read this. Call me at your earliest convenience although I suspect you have a welcoming party arranged. Enjoy it before we get to work. *TT.*

TEMPEST ALWAYS SIGNED off with *TT.* Viola had no idea what it represented. Perhaps her surname, perhaps it was some handle. It was a mystery, yet she was aware she was somehow protected by Tempest. All she had to fear was the level of danger the case might involve.

Once showered and dressed in a black pair of slacks and a white shirt, Viola was fresh and ready to meet her teaching peers. She picked up the school brochure from her desk when she heard a faint knocking on the door.

'Good morning, and welcome to Aurora Ms Bardo. Are you ready for a traditional Greek breakfast?' A smiling round-faced woman in a thin black cotton dress greeted her, 'I'm Maria the housekeeper of teacher accommodation, and the boarding house mistress.'

'Lovely to meet you, Maria, thank you for coming over. Yes, I look forward to a Greek breakfast this morning,' she lied when all she wanted was a gigantic mug of coffee, her morning ritual that she felt cheated out of today.' Are there many teachers in residence?'

'Now it is just you and an American gentleman, he's been here for three months. He is quiet, so don't fear any disturbance from him, an art teacher, but he's away this weekend, and will be back tomorrow night.'

Viola was pleased with Maria's open nature. She might call on her for a few favors when necessary, but with a level of caution. There was time yet. For now, she had to meet the Aurora staff.

THE DINING HALL was a long walk away from the cottages. The school spread across two side streets with one entrance at the back, and the other at the front through which she had entered the property.

A banquet table in the middle of the room was surrounded by small groups of teachers chatting and sipping hot drinks. Eyes turned in Viola's direction as she entered. Her ears burned and her heart skipped a little faster.

The table was laden with olives of every sort, and olive oil in large pouring urns, yoghurt and cold cuts, fruit, and pastries and a gigantic basket with fresh bread. A gentle sweet aroma hung in the air sending her tummy growling in pangs of delight.

Maria led her to the table and then to her seat next to the headmaster and his assistant. Miles clinked his glass with a teaspoon.

'Good morning all. Thank you for attending our breakfast on your down time weekend! Please join me in welcoming our well-traveled music specialist, Ms Bardo, from Australia!'

Viola blushed and secretly thanked her African ancestry for concealing her flush. Her curly hair and olive skin she inherited from her father. The deep brown, a mixture of her father's black hair and her mother's light brown hair. She shrunk beside the towering Miles who was smiling across the table at his staff. The staff muttered in soft tones with a hint of a musical lilt from some, 'Welcome Ms Bardo.' Viola felt the heat rise to her hairline when Miles announced, 'We have a celebrity among us, Ms Bardo has an album to her credit which we intend to showcase as a live rendition on one of our musical evenings.' She glanced around the room to ensure nobody thought she was claiming the limelight too soon. Instead, a loud round of applause followed, and a few younger teachers tapped the table in an appreciative drum roll. She wondered how Miles knew about her album, something she chose never to include in her teaching résumé.

Viola thanked the welcoming party and told them she was looking forward to getting to know them all. A white lie down and it was not yet midday!

ANOTHER MESSAGE from Tempest awaited her response.

Meet your contact in the CBD at 4:30 pm today over a cup of coffee. Keep it friendly. You will know what you need, for now, by the end of the meeting. Go to *Coffee Delight* on the main street, the contact will approach you with the usual code. I will be in touch tonight. *TT*.

3

Getting into town would not be easy, Viola had not driven a car in over a decade. A level of privacy was necessary, she had to find the options that would keep her comings and goings under the school's radar. In Australia she had her own apartment and was answerable to nobody. Here the community was privy to her movements. She had to ask Tempest at the right moment, why she wanted her to live at the teacher's residence at Aurora Academy.

Calling a cab could become a costly business by Sydney prices. She rifled through her handbag desperate for a crunch of peanut brittle. Thinking, plotting mode brought on the urge for her comfort treat. She tossed six bags of peanut brittle into her handbag when she left Sydney in the hope it would sustain her in Greece. Her nerves were jumpy whenever she was anticipating news or had a new mission lined up. The crunching reflex was something that developed from her father and his sister. Caramel popcorn was his fix-it for all pensive creative moments, something he prepared himself, to calm her too during her exam season, or when she had a spat with her best friend. Peanut brittle was her aunt's chicken soup to soothe a sad or ailing child. Now in her adult years she clung to the emotional satisfaction the sweet crunch offered and the warming memory of her father's care and her aunt's maternal nature. They were formidable role-models in her life, inspiring her to be her own person. Rolling the caramel flavored pieces in her mouth was her pondering necessity. Aha! She ripped open the bag of crispy, fresh, golden blocks of delight and cracked down hard on the first bite. It had hardened during air travel and had to breathe in warm air to soften a little. She put two bags into the fruit bowl on the kitchenette counter. The preparation of the peanut brittle with her aunt yielded serious conversations and uncontrollable laughter while roasting the nuts, then setting it aside to cool before adding it to a semi cool rich, dark caramel sauce. Her aunt's solution to all her childhood angst remained her emotional crutch.

She flicked through her phone searching for a taxi service close by when she noted that a bus service ran on a regular schedule from the main street. The brochure confirmed there was a bus pick-up point outside the main entrance. She had to speak to someone to verify if this was still operational as per the brochure. Maria, she envisioned, would ask too many questions, and what if she asked to go along with her as a tour guide! The best option was to ask the gatehouse security guard. It was his job to know everything that happened at the school. She picked up the telephone to ask him for his opinion; she hated being a newbie in these parts.

'Hello, Ms Bardo, yes, yes, the transport service is reliable, you can get the Athena ticket to go wherever you want here.' His deep, heavy voice helped her decide that she would rely on that service in Athens.

'Thank you, can I purchase that ticket here?'

'No, sorry, only at the metro in town, but we have a complimentary ticket with all your paperwork. If not, call Maria she can arrange it for you. My name is George, call anytime you require information. I am here most days and some nights. You will be well cared for here, Ms Bardo.' She felt uncomfortable hearing him say, 'you will be well cared for here.' It was rehearsed. Nothing was spontaneous.

'How long does it take to get to town, from here, George?'

'Fifteen minutes, not too long.'

From her trip to Bali she understood that local perceptions of travel time were way shorter than a foreigner's experience. She would leave an hour earlier to be sure she was punctual for her first meeting with god knows who.

The complimentary pre-paid ticket was in her desk drawer. If she got into the city earlier, she could take in the sights before she met the mystery person. Here she was at the center of democracy feeling a little lost and alienated. Work would soon consume her, being idle gave her too much head space for unnecessary thoughts including craving more peanut brittle!

George waved her off as she left. She was awestruck by the vision from the vantage of the bus. Mountains encircled the city giving it an enigmatic, majestic air. This was the city she longed to experience as a resident.

She got off, euphoric to be on the ground of the center of civilization. Some of the history she had learned and read in the books her mother had in the house. Plato, Aristotle, Socrates were on her mother's lips in the teaching of literature. It stirred her poetic muse; she had to answer the call, to pen a few lines in this majestic place. So much to see, and do, she had to fit it all in, somehow.

Syntagma Square was a landmark with plenty to mesmerize new eyes. Did Tempest have a specific reason for arranging her contact meeting here? She wandered along peering into shop windows and quickened her pace when she realized she had just fifteen minutes until her meeting.

Coffee Delight was quiet, two people sat up against the wall lost in conversation. A lone man was engrossed in a thick book.

Could it be him she wondered and hovered in the doorway when he looked up. Her father's tip on telepathy kicked in, she mentally chanted, *come to me if you are my contact.* It worked whenever she tried it on Champ, her Boston terrier, and her father, but never on her mother who was always a step ahead of her game. It worked! In an instant the man rose and approached her with a quizzical look, 'TTS33, Viola?' His eyes crinkled into slits when his cheeks puffed up as though he was certain it was her. It pleased her to hear him use her first name and Tempest's unique code for this operation.

He had a boyish look apart from the obvious gray strand that fell across his forehead. His penetrating black eyes, bright, large, unblinking buttons, fascinated her.

'Yes, TTV42,' she extended her hand, 'have you been waiting long?'

'I enjoy arriving half an hour earlier wherever I go. Sebastian, just Sebastian will do.' He reached out for her hand, 'Lovely to meet you, Viola. May I call you Viola?'

'I prefer being called by my first name. Hello *just* Sebastian. I'll remember to be half an hour early when we next meet. I was wandering around Syntagma Square, sorry.'

'No need to arrive early, I use my few stolen hours to catch up on reading. Do you enjoy reading?'

'Absolutely! It's the fuel that keeps me sane!' She laughed and he looked at her, scanning her face, noting her bounce of curly hair, and joyful manner.

'I have been instructed by Tempest that we should only meet outside of your school hours. Shall we decide where the best meeting place is to avoid being a familiar sight to curiosity? Would you like to sit and chat here today? They make the best coffee. I've had a cup already.'

'Oh, so you live in, Athens? I don't mind where we meet just so that it's not a deterrent to our work.'

'I am of Greek origin, I have some family living here, but I'm on sabbatical from my university contract in America. I was born there.'

'Interesting, we both come from traveling families who resettled elsewhere to their birth countries. What do you teach?'

'I am in the Educational Psychology Department and currently working on a research project. I would love to know about your background.'

'That's great, your skills are valuable to whatever case we are assigned.' She was not ready to reveal all about herself.

'And you're a music teacher so we are a good duet, I daresay, an ensemble of sorts.' His eyes gleamed under his generous long eyelashes.

She pondered on the cruelty of life, yet again here was a man with eyelashes that could offer adequate shade to his cheeks on a sunny day! The men she knew, including Rob Dwyer, had lush, long eyelashes, as did her father, but she inherited her sparse lashes from her mother. She needed thick layers of mascara to widen her eyes.

'Let's grab a takeaway cuppa and stroll down to the National Gardens to discuss what we're doing. This way we'll avoid any eavesdroppers.'

'That's a great idea!'

'We could go to my apartment. I've rented a place while I'm here.'

'The park sounds good today, I could use the walk, anyway,' Viola was not prepared to go to his apartment until she knew him well enough as someone with no agenda other than the assignment.

While walking to the National Park she asked, 'Have you met Tempest?'

'No, not in the flesh, she's just a voice and text message contact. I think it's the same for you.'

'Yes, I chat more to her though than text messaging. It's an odd relationship but one I have come to trust, value and respect. That must sound odd to you.'

'Not for a psychologist, women's intuition is something I don't doubt.'

'I have to be careful what I say to you.'

She found it easy to chat with Sebastian. His calm, jovial manner struck her. All she hoped for was that this is how he would always be in their interactions.

He said Tempest would call when they could talk without disturbance. Both were in the dark on the case they were to investigate. The Gardens were closing in an hour. They found a vacant park bench, he pulled out a small cell phone from his shirt pocket and handed her a tiny earpiece. She did not intend sitting close to him, something that made her awkward with strangers, but she had to shelve that reservation to maintain the privacy of Tempest's conversation. They had a job to do.

TEMPEST BUZZED.

Her calls came from different numbers. A melodic lilt popped into their ears.

'Viola, Sebastian, so glad you both found each other with no problems. Was the coffee good? That's the only place in the world where I savor it with delight. Hope you enjoyed my favorite.' She had a knack of making people comfortable.

After the pleasantries were over, she briefed them on the case. A six-year-old boy had been allegedly kidnapped from Germany. He was somewhere in Athens.

'The child is an Ambassador's son, so things could get tricky in our investigation. All I want from you both is the safe return of the child to his father. How you do this, is up to you. I am the messenger bringing forth new findings as it comes my way. A newly appointed family driver to a parliamentarian appears to be a suspect. He recently returned from Germany after many years there. He is not a Greek national but has worked in Greece before this chauffeur job. It's a delicate situation. The chauffeur's name is Matthew Soto, I don't have any photographs of him at this stage. We must find out if he has the child.'

'What time frame do we have on this?' Viola asked, concerned with the sketchiness of the details.

'Twelve days is all. Tread carefully and keep me updated several times in the day. Your safety is my prerogative too. Be warned that Matthew is an ex-military man, an injury changed his lifestyle.'

'Any idea at what location he served?' Sebastian asked.

'Afghanistan. He has a limp on his left side, presumably from the bullet that was lodged in the hip.'

'Are there any clues on the parliamentarian he's serving as a chauffeur?'

'Later, on that, for now gather as much as you can, twelve days. I'll be in touch.' She left them to mull over how they would proceed.

'We better get out of here, the gates close soon, it's a bit of a hike to the entrance.'

'I'll do the pre-investigation while you are at work and we can continue in the evening. We have a tight deadline.'

She was uneasy that he assumed what he would do without consultation. For now, she would let that pass. What he did not know about her was that she was a combination of hard-nosed determination and tranquility. He dared not cross her!

She caught the bus, refusing a ride in his hired car, and headed back to her new home. Anonymity was not negotiable with a little boy at risk.

The thing that troubled her was how did Tempest know to call them at the precise moment they sat on the park bench.

4

It was nine o'clock when she got back to her little cottage. A different guard was at the gate. He expected her to sign in, looked at her teacher identification card and nodded with not a word uttered. Security was tight at Aurora Academy compared to Blackwater Ridge Performing Arts Academy. Now she had to accept that her every move would be questioned.

With international Ambassadors' children at the school, she understood the need for this level of security. Were day staff who lived off campus subjected to the same checks?

She sauntered back to her cottage, exhausted from the day's happenings. The lights two doors down from her told her the American must be back from his weekend away. She pondered when she would meet him.

Viola was not on class in the morning. Jace Dimakos was conducting an orientation program with her until midday. A hot bath before bed was what she needed to soothe her tired body and overactive mind. The internal telephone line chimed at her desk. She had half a mind to let it ring out when she realized she was in a new place and answerable to her host. An anxious Maria was on the line.

'Hello Ms Bardo, is everything okay? I noticed you were out this evening when I came over to see if you needed anything, before I retired for the night.'

She sighed, the first signs were seeping through, if anyone would pry into her affairs it would be Maria.

'Thank you. I went into town to take in a few sights before the school week started. It's pretty easy to get to places with the bus system here.'

'That's good! Athens is a safe place, so you must enjoy as much as you can. If you want some insider tips on shopping and cuisine, don't hesitate to ask. Rest well, Ms Bardo, you have a big day tomorrow.'

'Thank you, that's really kind of you, I might come to you when in doubt. Rest well, too, and sorry for keeping you up. Please call me Viola, no need for any formality.' Viola was unsure if Maria heard her apology, the line was dead. She felt dreadful for thinking the housekeeper was a prying old biddy, she was just a caring soul who wanted her to be happy during her stay at Aurora. Lying in a warm bath had her wondering about Maria's role in the school, she seemed subservient in her urgency to please. She speculated if this was an inherent personal attribute, or whether the school created this expectation. Oh well tomorrow will shed fresh light on the school in operation. Then there was Sebastian, he seemed nice enough, a little controlling perhaps, or did he think he was doing her a favor by taking on a self-proclaimed lead in an investigation that was not off the ground yet. She felt a tinge of warmth towards Sebastian, her only certain ally at this stage. Miles and Jace were enigmas with their egos and insecurity. Saying little, yet saying so much. Miles tried hard to convince her that Aurora was a prestigious school but a laid-back place for staff.

The gatehouse signing in process and Maria's falling over herself pleasing attitude did not sit well with her. She had to toss out these negative thoughts. Once they took seed it would be difficult to obliterate, defining everything thereafter.

The case Tempest presented of a child in a desperate situation made her realize that she had to maintain a clear head throughout the investigation. She closed her eyes to summon a visual sense of where the child might be. Her phone buzzed on the vanity top, she stretched over to grab it. It had to be Tempest. It was from an unlisted number.

'Sorry to disturb you, are you settling down on your first night?'

'Not quite, perhaps in an hour or so, do you have more news?'

'What's the prognosis on Sebastian? Think you can work with him on this case?'

Tempest's abrupt manner startled her.

'He appears to be someone I could work with. He wants the lion share of the job, I think. Any reason for asking?' Viola knew she might not get an answer but pushed the button, anyway.

'Beware, Viola, don't give him the upper-hand, you both need to work on this together, and there is method in my madness in putting you two together on this. I would prefer you to lead the way to the recovery of the boy, but for now, I will leave it as it is, both working in harmony.' That strangling comment added to Viola's burden on who was who in this merry-go-round of strange encounters.

'Do you have more information to add?' Viola coughed and paused.

She knew by Tempest's momentary silence that the question annoyed her. While she worked out how to reframe what was on her mind, Tempest added a vital piece of information.

'The child has high levels of anxiety and has had a seizure

once which adds a deeper level of care. Emotional triggers might set him off. I will pass on the medical rap once the father hands it over. The boy's English skills are limited. You might struggle to communicate with him, but I know I can count on you to overcome this.'

'I have a basic proficiency in German, which might help. More on the child's medical history is important.'

'Yes, I am trying to get that across to you as soon as possible. While you are teaching, I can communicate with Sebastian if more information surfaces. I will copy you into all discussions and sharing of information, it's just that you might get to it later than Sebastian. Twelve days is all we have.' She hung up.

Lovely, there's not enough to go on! Viola reached for the peanut brittle. Her incognito investigation needed a crunch reflex to set the process in motion. Making a mental note or using her coding system was imperative with just twelve days to achieve the goal. Her poetry coding system worked well in English, French, and Portuguese to guide her mental note making. The joy of being raised multi-lingual! She had to brush up on her German soon. She felt an overwhelming urge to write and grabbed her secret work journal and penned:

> *Little boy lost*
> *In a vast metropolis*
> *Centre of history and culture*
> *Who is the obscene vulture?*
> *That has stolen your joy.*

Telling lines had to be erased and committed to memory.

THE GENEROUS BED and soft velvety covers curled around her. She dozed off for an hour and awoke with a dry burning sensation in her throat. She jumped out of bed and had to steady herself on the bedside table. The room spun at dizzying speed. She sat down and waited for it to stop. Oh no! I can't have this happening now! Not on the eve of my first day on the job! After the dizziness subsided, she poured herself a glass of chilled water and added a splash of lemon. Kind, thoughtful, Maria left fruit and salad greens in her fridge. She caught a few hours of sleep and rose at 7 am to get ready to meet Jace in the school conference room for a briefing and a tour of the school before she met her class. Brewed coffee is what she needed to jolt her senses and clear her head. With black pants, black shoes and a white blouse thrown on, she pinned her hair up, put on her large hoop earrings, flung a water bottle and peanut brittle into her bag and headed to the conference room. The campus was still at 8:45 am, not a person nor a bird stirred.

A smiling Jace Dimakos greeted her, 'I trust you rested well, you look fresh and ready to claim the day.'

If only he knew that a little eyeshadow worked wonders!

'Good morning, yes, thank you I did? Do I address you as Jace or do we remain formal at all times?'

'Formal greeting around students and at staff gatherings, but in private conversations I'm Jace.' He flashed her an awkward grin, then stopped himself with a quick head shake, leaving her thinking that he was more restrained than the housekeeper. Miles Alexakis was meeting prospective parents for whom lunch was served in his private quarters. Viola had to come to terms with the top-notch she would hobnob around — something she was not looking forward to. What would the students be like?

The librarian was a bubbly woman on any good day, now she held her enthusiasm in check with frequent glances shot at Jace.

'Please come over any time, we are open some evenings if you would like to select some private reading, or if you need any books for your teaching. Please let me know and I'll get them in for you.'

'Thank you, please call me Viola.'

She nodded and looked at Jace again.

'We must move along to your class now,' Jace urged, leaving the librarian with a hesitant shadow of a smile as she watched them leave.

'Thank you, I will be in to trouble you for some personal reading.' Viola smiled with a cheery wave and thought she heard her say, 'No trouble at all.'

'YOUR GROUP IS 9B —'B' for Bardo, students are on their way.

'Did you change the class designation to suit my arrival?'

Jace laughed for the first time, 'I wish I could take credit for that, but you are replacing a Mr Benson so that made it easy.'

'Ah, I see. Well, that worked out fine. Is he an Englishman? His name makes me think he is although I could be wrong.'

'He's Greek, born and raised here, but abroad on an exchange program. It is his first trip out of Greece. He's a recent graduate.'

'Are there behavioral problems in 9B that I should be alerted to? Or health issues?'

'Get to know them first, and you decide, I'll meet you again at the end of the week for a follow-up.' His sudden officious attitude left her dumbstruck. She saw her class marching towards her room, looking at each other and whispering once they noticed her standing next to the assistant head. Fifteen students sang, 'Good morning, Mr Dimakos.' Some nodded to acknowledge Viola's presence.

'Take your seats students, once you settle, please welcome Ms Bardo, your current replacement music teacher. Students clapped and shouted out, 'Welcome, Ms Bardo!' Viola was not used to seeing high school students this docile. She detested being referred to as a *replacement*, but had to swallow her pride, she was a foreigner here after all. Jace summoned the captain to make a welcome speech. A tall, smiling girl stepped to the front of the room.

'Ms Bardo, we are excited to have you as our teacher this term, we hope your stay is an enjoyable one. We look forward to hearing about Australia. 9B has something for you, she turned and nodded to a girl in the back row. The girl stood up, opened the door at the rear of the classroom and walked towards Viola with a gigantic bunch of red roses.

'For you, you are our rose from Australia.' The class giggled, and some clapped while looking at the assistant headmaster for his reaction.

'Thank you so much, you really did not have to do this, but thank you, it will brighten up my desk and keep me in a good mood. Be careful I might not want to leave!' The class laughed and Jace blushed.

The girl with the bouquet said, 'Mr Dimakos bought the flowers and told us to give it to you.'

Jace's red face was difficult to conceal but he managed a feeble smile.

'It's part of our school's welcome gesture... I hope you like them...'

Viola thanked him and the students as he rushed out the room.

HER FIRST TEACHING day at Aurora was a pleasant one with no room to think about why she received such a massive bouquet of roses.

By 3:15 pm she was back in her cottage and starving! She missed lunch in the staff canteen, and all she had, was fruit and a few tomatoes and lettuce leaves in the fridge. A quick call to Maria and, in a short space of time, a plate of sandwiches arrived at her door. Part of her thought this could be a good life, but she cautioned herself to drop the notion.

She scrolled through her text messages. At 1 pm Sebastian asked her to contact him.

This was the beginning of her clandestine days at Aurora.

5

The flowers brought a welcome fragrance and a brilliant splash of color to her brown and gray surroundings. Her desk was inviting and piqued her creative juices. Her personal poetry notebook had no recent entry. Thoughts of Jace's awkward, bashful acknowledgment of having purchased the welcome flowers bothered her. Why buy it in the first place if it made him uncomfortable? He was a strange man, and in her book, this overstepped the professional line in using her class as a cover for his personal aims. Her students were oblivious in their innocence to being used. Or were they polite as Aurora expected and did as they were told? She picked up a pen and scribbled.

Flowers of delight
Create fragrant brilliant light
The strange giver is shy
I wonder why
Stumbling fumbling and odd
Oh, what a darn sod!

SHE LAUGHED and folded the page to hide her impulsive composition reminding herself that she should be grateful. Lord knows she had this drilled into her as a child, 'Mind your manners, Viola, did you say thank-you Viola? Have I not taught you to be polite child... be grateful child... nobody owes you anything child... remember that!'

A FAINT KNOCK at the door disturbed her memories. It was five o' clock and the school grounds were deserted. At Blackwater teachers worked up to five-thirty preparing for the next day's lessons or teaching after school classes. She peered through the peep-hole. A wiry, tall, scraggly bearded man stood on her verandah. Perhaps he was a new gate-house attendant. Why would he want to see her?

Her nervousness was soon quelled when the man introduced himself as Vince, the American from next door.

'Ms Bardo, I hope you don't mind my intrusion. We are the only two teachers in residence, so I figured I better come over to meet you.' He curled his lower lip in mock apology. Viola liked his openness and felt instantly happy to meet him.

'Please come in, lovely to meet you, Vince. No formalities please, I'm plain old Viola!' she laughed and led him in.

'Glad we're on the same page with that. Formality makes me tense. How are you settling in?'

'I love the tranquility, and everybody has been overwhelmingly hospitable which I'm not used to but it's lovely to feel welcomed. Maria told me you were the American art teacher on exchange here. Which state do you hail from?'

'New York, Brooklyn kid, born and bred. How about you? Which part of Australia?'

'Sydney, although I barely spend more than a few months

at a time there. I like to think of myself as a global citizen. Have you been to Australia? It's an amazing country.'

She poured Vince a cup of coffee and offered him a piece of peanut brittle.

'Haven't been Down Under yet, but it's on the cards for my next exchange position. How long will you be here?'

'It's a short stint on this contract, six weeks, I usually do six months at a time in different countries.'

'That is short! I'm here for the year. My leap of faith. I needed change with all that has gone on in my world, so this is right. I should leave you to get on with your work but remember I'm here. Come over any time. Great to meet you, Viola!'

'Thank you for coming over. Good to know I have a friendly neighbor.'

She watched him leave, pleased that she had another person to call a friend at Aurora. If Jace was strange, then Vince was a down to earth, regular guy, a friend that every girl needs without emotional baggage.

A missed call from an unknown number told her Tempest was trying to reach her. There was no way of calling back. There was no safe number this time like she had on her previous assignment.

Viola called Sebastian.

'I'm glad you called. Tempest has information to impart. Where can I meet you?'

'I can get to you by eight, it's best that you don't come around here, just yet. Is that a suitable time?'

'Can you make it earlier, come over to my place, I'll cook dinner.'

'There's school prep to organize and the boarding house will be settled by eight for the evening. This way I can avoid detection by a curious, roaming teenager. Don't worry about dinner, we could meet at the cafe in Syntagma again.'

'I have to make dinner for myself, meet me here for Tempest's call and we could walk over to the cafe after that if you're up for a late coffee.'

'Sounds like a plan, see you at eight. I am on study duty on Thursday evenings in the library so I will be unreachable between seven to nine-thirty.'

'Thanks for letting me know, we should pass this info onto Tempest too.'

'Great, I have a bit of information to share so it might be better to meet at your place.'

GEORGE WAS on gatehouse duty that evening much to Viola's relief.

'Good evening, Ms Bardo. Lovely evening for a stroll or jog. Good to see you are very much a local already.' He laughed and did not ask when she would return.

'It sure is a lovely evening, will you be on duty when I return?'

'All night Ms Bardo. It's my night shift week.'

Viola made a note to remember the sequence of George's night shifts. Her life was easier with him on duty.

As she walked along, she had the wild urge to pull out a piece of peanut brittle from her pocket and thought it unwise. Her front tooth was a little worse for wear and had to stay intact until she could visit her dentist in Sydney.

She hopped on a bus surprised at herself that she agreed to meet Sebastian this soon at his apartment. She arrived two minutes before eight.

'Right on schoolteacher time!' Sebastian teased now that he had a sense of her personality and humor.

'Yes, it's in my blood, not forgetting that my mother is a stickler for punctuality. She says it has nothing to do with her

French or African halves but must be somewhere from her unknown British ancestry!'

'Your mother sounds like an interesting person. What a great life with rich cultures on both sides of your gene pool.'

Viola rolled her eyes, chuckled, and bowed, 'Hmmm, as you say, Sebastian, sir, but live the life first!'

'You are going to love this, I have grilled sardines and potatoes just the way the Portuguese make it, care to join me for dinner?'

'Sardines! Well, I will have a taste of your fine cooking. This will impress my father.'

Sebastian, tempted to grab the moment for a tease asked, 'So did your boyfriends have to go through daddy's test first before they got too close to you?'

'No way! My father is the coolest man you will ever meet. My school mates adored him. I hope you meet him someday.'

He saw the child who idolized her father in those lines and envied that love and loyalty.

'Now back to business. Tempest says the driver who allegedly kidnapped the little boy is the brother-in-law of the German Ambassador. His sister was married to the Ambassador. She died eighteen months ago.'

'So, we are unsure whose child has been kidnapped? The driver's or the Ambassador's? I need some clarity on this.'

'The Ambassador's, and *driver's sister's* only child.'

'Aha! The plot thickens! A personal family vendetta perhaps? Let us hope he has no intention of harming the child if it's his nephew.'

'I don't mean to burst your bubble, remember Richard of Gloucester and the winter of his discontent. That guy left a huge impact on me during my school days. I could not understand why he was so brutal to his nephews.'

'Why ruin this hope? Men! At least Shakespeare got it right!'

'Now I know why Tempest attached me to you, and not a man in this investigation. When children are involved, emotions are essential.'

'That is not Tempest's reason, perhaps yours? My emotions are always in control. I make sure of that.'

Sebastian laughed and walked up to the kitchen counter to pour them each a glass of wine.

'Nothing for me, please, it's a school night.'

He held off insisting she have a drink.

'I spent my day circling around the parliamentary building. There's a wall around the entire circumference. We must get inside on one of those tours, there's one on Saturday morning at 10 am. Are you free then? Two sets of eyes will be better.'

'Yes count me in.'

Tempest called at the exact time she said she would.

'Good evening. The driver, Matthew Soto, the brother-in-law of the German Ambassador, works in a personal capacity for the Prime Minister's family, transporting his children to and from school and running other domestic errands. Your mission in finding the child is also to assess whether Mr Soto has any political aspirations. I recommend that you tail him tomorrow, Sebastian. He drives a black Mercedes C-Class sedan.'

'Thanks, got that.'

'This situation complicates our investigation because he is inside the Prime Minister's private life. At this stage the PM is ignorant of his German connection to the abducted child. An airport contact has footage with Soto arriving a month ago holding the hand of a child.'

'The child might be happy to be with him if he is a known relative.' Viola interjected.

'Yes, but we are to focus on the domestic issue on hand. The protection of the child is not a political matter and I assure you, your safety in Athens is paramount while you work for my organization.'

'Thank you, Tempest,' they chorused in docile unison.

'You are down to eleven days. Get to it then.'

She clicked off.

'Our Tempest, warm and fuzzy one second and issuing non-negotiable orders the next.' Sebastian grinned.

'That's the nature of the job! She's given us a lot to go on. Now let's plan the next step. I have an hour for a reasonable schoolteacher return to the residence.'

'I'll trail Soto tomorrow and you can meet me at Syntagma Square after school tomorrow evening around six.'

'I can't. I have study duty tomorrow evening, remember?'

'Can you swap the day?'

'I'll try but can't guarantee it will be possible.'

'Let me know and we can move faster on this. Eleven days and the clock's ticking.'

'The additional issue is that the child has had a seizure and stress is likely to worsen this.'

'I suspect the child is happy but might pine for his father. That's just my hopeful speculation, we need the facts now on the child's wellbeing.'

Viola grabbed the bag of peanut brittle from her jacket pocket and offered Sebastian a piece.

'No thank you, I value my teeth. I had them capped before I came out on this sabbatical.'

Viola knew her partner was a glamour boy. He dressed in name brand shoes and pants and smelt like he'd bathed in exotic perfume. He was neat like no man she knew. Her father was an artist who walked around with specks of paint on his nose and hands and sometimes streaked across his forehead. Sebastian knew how to look after himself. But he had no romantic connections, or so it seemed.

* * *

BACK AT AURORA, George was following a radio commentary on British football.

'Good evening Ms Bardo, did you enjoy your stroll?'

'Thank you, George, I did. I jogged more than I strolled.' Telling little white lies was part of the package in her role as investigator for Tempest.

She walked to the American's door. It was time to ask for a favor. Music wafted from under Vince's front door. Viola hesitated and tapped once. The door eased open and Vince stood before her in a long blue robe surrounded by puffs of smoke emitted from the incense burner he was holding in his right hand.

'I'm so sorry to have disturbed you. I can come back later.'

'What a pleasant surprise, come in, I have just finished my meditation. My ritual before I get down to writing or drawing.'

'Are you sure?'

'A hundred percent, care for a cup of green tea?'

'Perhaps, later. What do you write?'

'Crime fiction, I've started my second book.'

'How wonderful, I'd love to hear all about it. I dabble in poetry a bit. It's my soothing space.'

'Wonderful! We'll have much to share.'

'Look, the reason for my late-night visit is that I need a favor. You can say no if you are busy.'

'I'm listening, what is it?'

She explained that she needed cover for her study supervision the next evening and that she would cover a double session for him.

'Desperate!' Vince laughed waving smoke away from his face. 'I should put this down before I asphyxiate myself! Sure, I'll cover for you and beware I might just hold you to the promise of two for the price of one!'

'Thank you so much.'

'I'm kidding about the double session. Hope you know that.'

'Thank you, Vince, I appreciate your assistance.'

'Study supervision is the easiest especially when it's maths night. It's Greek to me so I get to write in another chapter on my story. The kids understand I can't answer any of their questions!'

'You keep me sane around here with your earthy sense of humor!'

She thanked him and dashed back to her quarters.

THAT NIGHT VIOLA had a vivid dream of running down Syntagma Square chasing a child who was too fast for her. The child turned around at every corner and gave her a cheeky grin. The faster she ran the further away the child got until he vanished before her eyes. She heard Tempest's hollow warning.

Eleven days, that's all you have, eleven days.

6

Viola met Sebastian at a tucked away, quaint patisserie in Syntagma Square. The need to remain ghostly figures was paramount to achieving their ends. He teased her for being punctual, and here he was with his nose in a book again waiting for her, and she was ten minutes early! Her temptation was difficult to resist.

'Hello sir! You must have been a schoolteacher in your last life! Or has university life given you the edge on punctuality?'

'It has to be something in my ancestry too, perhaps on *my* British side! Did you have a good day?'

'You don't miss a moment for a laugh! Yes, my day was good but right now I'm anxious with ten days left to find the child. My sleep was disturbed by visions of a child running away from me. I'm exhausted. Syntagma is taking a dark turn in my dreams!'

'At least it's just a dream. I have a lot to tell you.'

'Did you follow the driver all day?'

'I started early in the day and followed him from the moment he left the PM's house with the children. He dropped off two children, a boy and a girl perhaps aged eight and ten at a local primary school, but here is the interesting thing — he left the eldest boy, the third child, at Aurora Academy! He could be around fourteen or fifteen, a tall, lean lad.'

Snap! Crunch! Crack! Viola bit off a piece of peanut brittle.

'Wow! Did you break a tooth! That was loud.'

'No, I don't think so. This investigation is getting under my skin. Do you have any photos of the children?'

'I do have a few on my phone, but are you sure you did not crack a tooth?'

'No, I haven't. The teenager could be in one of my classes. This might complicate my life with him being the PM's son and me the investigator of an abduction involving one of his father's trusted staff.'

'Allegedly involving, even though Tempest says it was the driver. We're not sure on that yet. The boy will not be a deterrent to our investigation, but you could use your situation to our advantage by listening in to his conversations. Assuming that you do teach him.'

'I'm not comfortable doing that — we have strict laws in Australia about student privacy, so I have to be careful.'

'Not invading the boy's privacy but a bit of harmless sleuthing around him is all.'

'How?'

'I'll leave you to figure that out. I will continue the outside investigation by following Matthew Soto.'

'I could question Vince and Maria without creating suspicion. They are the two people who might assist. I know that foreign Ambassadors' and local politicians' kids are given a pseudonym for their privacy and protection.'

'That might hinder you.'

'Why are you smiling?'

'I think I have just what you need.'

'And pray what is that?'

Viola took a large bite of peanut brittle and yelped.

'Oh no! Now I have broken a filling!'

'I knew that would happen. You must toss this habit. You could end up wearing dentures sooner than you think.'

His relaxed mood irritated her, she was anxious about their tight time frame and now she had a broken filling on the upper right side smack in the middle of her smile line! How was she going to get to a dentist when so much was going on?

'Dentures! I would prefer implants and look at your stunning smile. I will end up looking like an exhumed corpse with these teeth! You're right, I need to kick this habit! It's as bad as being a smoker!'

Sebastian enjoyed hearing Viola give in to his suggestion.

'My plan for tomorrow is to get inside the house.'

'The PM's house? That's dangerous, he will have security teeming at his place.'

'I meant Matthew Soto's place. He has a walking cane. I saw him get out the car to remove a school project from the boot for one of the younger children. That must be as a result of the hip injury Tempest mentioned. I detected a limp, so he won't be quick on his feet but he's stocky with bodybuilder pectorals! He could take me out I think.'

'We have to tread with care. I don't think you should attempt going inside his home. We cannot incur injuries with the limited days we have.'

'I have to do this with a watertight plan.'

'While you do that, I will have to find a dentist. I'm not sure if this classifies as a work injury!'

'Ask Tempest, she might know a dentist here.'

'Are you kidding me? I am too embarrassed for her to know my weakness. A fixation on peanut brittle!'

'Don't be surprised, I think she knows about your secret! I haven't had dinner yet, have you? Your pastry is untouched. There's a gourmet pizza place in the next street that has an extensive range on offer.'

'Pizza will be a soft option for my fragile teeth this evening. I need some groceries too, and we should update Tempest on our next move. I need approval from her to talk to the PM's boy. Mind you, I'm not at all comfortable using a child to gain information. I have no idea who the kid is at this stage.'

Sebastian handed her his phone to message Tempest with their latest plans. His laid-back manner was more prevalent since trust had developed between them. He wanted her to feel relaxed and toyed with thoughts of schoolteachers being anxious about their performance on the job. The accountability that teaching demanded was something he knew well with his father being a primary educator. What would a tense Viola be like as a music teacher brought hilarious visions to mind which he knew he could not share with her? Not now. She was passionate and teaching jokes around her specialist area might not go down too well. He had to remember that she had a sensitive side.

'Did I tell you my father,' he hesitated, 'was a primary school teacher? He used to say he was married to his job. Everything revolved around his preparation schedule, he switched off the television after dinner, and I had to be reading in my room. He loved his work, but sadly that was his only passion.'

'I am passionate about teaching but it's not my sole love as I'm here aren't I? Justice comes close to that passion, but I agree that trying to maintain commitment to anything else is a huge stretch.'

Sebastian sensed her reluctance to say more about herself but she questioned him.

'Is being a university professor your only love?'

'It is, but like you, I'm passionate about social and criminal justice matters.'

He offered to drop her off close to the school. To his surprise, she accepted after she purchased a few grocery items from a convenience store close to his apartment.

That night Viola packed the fridge with her convenience meals tucking them to the back in the hope that Maria would not know about her quick-fix meals. Then she scrolled through the school portal, searching for any information to lead her closer to returning the abducted boy to his father. She had no idea who the PM's son was, and looking for him with no sense of his appearance, would be a wasted exercise. A quick message to Sebastian and she had footage of the boy getting out of Matthew Soto's car. It was a distant image of the boy but if she studied it long enough, she would make the connection when she saw him the next day.

NINE DAYS TO go and a live contact was in her classroom. She rose early and baked a batch of cheese muffins. These were gentle on her teeth, and they were quick and easy to prepare. She wrapped four muffins in a paper napkin and left them at Vince's front door.

When she was excited or nervous her body movements were erratic, darting from one activity to the next. She stepped into her work shoes when she heard a rat-a-tat-tat on her door. A smiling Vince was chewing on a buttered cheese muffin with a coffee mug in his other hand.

'Look at you, like a content kitten.'

'These are delicious, a cloud of heaven in every bite! Thank you! Feels like being back in my childhood home!'

'You too! I have so many memories around the smell and taste of these delights. I think I needed the comfort of home.'

Vince frowned, cocked his head to one side, 'You were out late last night.'

'Hey! Are you stalking me, officer? Your door knocking had me thinking it was the law calling!'

They both laughed and Viola pounced on the moment, 'Vince, do you think I teach any Ambassador's children?'

'Yeah, you have the PM's child in 9SG.'

'Really? Who is the class teacher?'

'Sergei Giovanni, the science man, have you met him?'

'How do you know this with the tight protocol around here? No, I haven't met him yet.'

'I pry with innocent, curious talk. Why the interest?'

'Yeah, you're good at this innocent, curious talk, I see.'

She told him she was with a friend the night before, a local who told her the school enrolled many politicians' children. Vince was not familiar with the student but had heard that he was in 9SG and knew he was a tall, lean boy with a mop of dark brown curly hair. A staff member pointed him out on the school oval.

'Some teachers do talk around here but the boy's just the PM's offspring, no relative of God you know!' Vince was an art teacher with a passion for literature. He enjoyed reading everything he could find on power and politics. He thanked her for the muffins and offered to cook her dinner one night.

'I might take you up on that. Have a good day,' she called after him. He dipped in a low bow as if accepting the applause for his theatrical performance. Vince made Aurora normal and human.

She replayed the video Sebastian sent her and decided she would observe the boy that day.

AT 10:30 am 9SG lined up outside her music room door. A tall, lanky boy straggled to the back of the line. A wild rush of curls bobbed on his head to his rhythmic gait. She knew it was him. He looked at her with a half apologetic, half cheeky grin, 'Hey Ms Bardo, sorry I'm a little late. Mr Alexakis wanted to see me.'

'That's okay, let's hurry in. What's our name, again?'

'Brendon, Brendon Sanchez, Ms.'

What a load of rubbish! But she had a name even if it was a fake one.

The choir took up their position, and those not selected tried their hand at the instrument they were still learning to play. The cacophony of sounds disturbed the choir, and Viola stopped Brendon's overzealous attempt at strumming a guitar. She had to stop her own enjoyable piano playing. Thoughts on whether the PM attended show night intrigued her. The boy's keenness to play the guitar was a way to get to know him.

Sebastian was out on his investigative mission that afternoon when Tempest called Viola.

'Monitor that Sanchez kid, listen to his conversations, observe his movements, but never forget that while you are at Aurora, you are an educator. Duty of care must come first.' Her diligence on doing things the right way appealed to Viola. Placido Bardo, her father, was inclined to float around responsibility issues, her mother was upright on such matters when it suited her. As much as she denied it, she was her mother's daughter when it came to rules.

BRANDON SANCHEZ WAS A WELL-MANNERED boy with an easy disposition. She had to get him to open up to her soon.

He was a necessary link in the investigation.

7

A nd then there were eight days.

It was Friday and a relaxed air pervaded the campus. Miles Alexakis was out of town at a principals' conference. Ineffectual, timid Jace was at the helm. Staff dress slipped a notch reminding Viola of mufti-day in Australia where students donned their casual wear for a gold coin collection to raise funds for a charity of choice. Today students went about their business as usual, unaware that the headmaster was out of town. He had days where he locked himself in his ivory tower and nobody saw nor heard from him. Her Australian headmaster was different, Rob was a people person most of the time except when he was nursing the bruises of criticism from some quarters of his staff. Then he sealed himself off in his office. Often, they were criticisms he did not deserve.

Viola had a 10 am start that morning and called her father before she headed to class. Her mother was hard to track with her hectic schedule. The time difference was not an issue with an hour between them while she was in Athens. If she needed pampering, she turned to her father.

'Viola! Artista! Lovely to hear your voice! Her father's warm, crooning caramel tone was the music of her childhood in her ears.

'Papa, it's so good to hear you too. How are you? Are you getting enough sleep?'

'Artista! Artista! Don't worry your musical head over me, baby girl! I am just an old man but ever so happy to hear from you. I worry about you jumping from country to country. But how are things with you?'

She loved the way her father never pronounced the 'h' sound when he said, 'how are things with you.' The major part of her life growing up with her father did not influence imbibing the nuances of his pronunciation and language choices. She was as Aussie as could be, drawing out the vowel sounds, particularly the 'a' sound while her father clipped every vowel sound.

'I am working through my mission here. The school is good to me. I am happy, papa. It will please you to know I made a few friends already.'

'Wonderful, Artista! Everybody loves you. Did you hear from your mother?'

She knew that question was coming. Her father had no communication with her mother and relied on her to update him. For all their years apart, he never stopped loving her.

'No, papa. I've been busy and will call her soon. The time difference is good while I am here.'

'Artista, I asked if you heard from your mother, not when you will call her, *meu filho*.'

The only bitterness her father carried against her mother was that she abandoned her little girl to pursue a career. He was both mother and father to his darling Artista, and his sister, Lorenza helped him whenever she could, but she was young and had her own life. She disappeared when Viola was nine, leaving her father with the hardest blow to bear — gone with not a whisper, presumed dead. A life size painting of his beloved sister adorned the entrance to his gallery in Portugal.

'I'm not fussed, if mother does not call, papa. I know her life is busy. Now you don't worry your wise artistic head over that.'

That was their major connection not just as father and daughter but as one respected artist to another. It hurt her when her mother referred to her ex-husband as an idle aging artist — something she never told her father. Every time she told him not to worry his wise artistic head, his response was, 'Now you sound like your mother.' While the bitterness lingered beneath the surface, the love he had for his ex-wife lived deep under his skin.

'So, are you coming to Portugal for Christmas? One week with me, right, Artista?' She heard his anxiety, he wanted confirmation each time he spoke to her that she would come to him. Aging brought such loneliness to a man who had hordes of people hanging onto him during the years when he threw money at every struggling artist he met. Now his gallery had much competition, keeping it open was a huge financial burden, but he loved his work and would continue to run it with a few trusted people.

'I hope that it will be possible. Leave it with me, I have a knack of having my way,' she laughed.

'Wonderful, Artista! Now tell me, your mission will be a win-win, right?'

'I hope so, papa, I hope so.'

After her chat with her beloved papa, Viola sent her mother a message and confirmed they would chat the next morning. Her mother never initiated contact. She met and married a mathematics professor at the university in Cape Town. Now her life was preoccupied with university dinners and ballroom dancing lessons the professor enjoyed.

Her mother had moved on, but grief, loss, and undying love trapped her father.

* * *

MARIA CAME OVER AROUND 9 am bearing a large watermelon gift.

'How lovely of you, Maria! You are always looking after me. Thank you!'

'Ms Bardo, it makes me happy that you appreciate and enjoy the little things I bring to you.'

'I must cook you a special meal soon. I can cook, well so my father tells me.'

'No need for that, Ms Bardo, there is enough to do each day, and if I can ease a day here and there for you, I will.'

Viola reached out and squeezed Maria's arm. She warmed a cheese muffin in the microwave and brewed a cup of coffee for her special guest.

'Ooh that smells delicious, what is it?' Maria rubbed her hands together.

'Cheese muffins just as my aunt made them. If you want the recipe, I'm sure she will be happy for you to have it.' They laughed as old friends do, sharing kitchen secrets.

'You are close to your aunt, I sense that. Ah, I see you have a well-stocked fridge, so we can expect to smell your cooking wafting around the school.'

Viola smiled and did not go into her closeness with Lorenza as a cordial mood settled around them. She knew she had to ask a few questions before she headed off to her class.

'How long have you been working at Aurora?'

'Oh Lord, a long time now. Let me see,' Maria looked up at the ceiling searching for a timespan, counting on her fingers. 'Twenty-five years coming up next year.'

'So, you are part of the history of this school. Have you always been a boarding house mistress?'

'Yes, yes, same role, for as long as that. I enjoy working with the boarders and being of help to exchange teachers that come over. The overseas students pine for their families, especially for their mothers, so I try to narrow that gap for them, you know.'

'That's wonderful! Are there many day students?'

'Just a few, but those whose parents travel overseas sometimes on work matters, come in as temporary boarders while their parents are away. They are generally the children of politicians.'

Maria led Viola where she wanted to go with the next provocative question.

'Does Aurora have more international or local politicians' kids?'

'A balance, I think. You are teaching the Prime Minister's son, although you won't know that because they go under a different name for security reasons. Some have a bodyguard around but none of us know who they are. Maybe even incognito as teachers. I've talked too much now.'

'I won't say a word.' Viola felt guilty for the cheese muffin seduction. Her ears burned when Maria mentioned incognito teachers. Her legitimate role was as a qualified teacher, her private investigator side had nothing to do with being a teacher. That's what she preferred to think.

'I know you are trustworthy Ms Bardo. It shows in your eyes. I never trust people who cannot look me in the eye when they speak to me. There is an openness about you.'

Viola brushed aside her guilt, 'My mother says I am as tight as a bank vault when there's somebody's secret in my heart.'

Maria clapped her hands and threw her head back in a raspy laugh, 'What secrets were you keeping from your precious mama?'

'Being an only child of divorced parents was a tricky situation. I never carried tales across both houses. This way I showed them that I loved them equally. Just the way children should love their parents. Nothing will make me wilfully destroy my relationship with either of them.'

'You know, Viola — now I feel comfortable to call you by your first name because if I had a child, I would want her to have your kindness.'

'You would be an amazing mother, Maria.'

'Mother to all, the help is all I am.'

'Never the help as you say, you are a warm and generous soul and that is why Aurora has you as the leading border mistress all these years. Miles speaks well of you.'

The twinkle in Maria's eyes was special. Viola knew that praise was not what she wanted. She enjoyed making others happy, that was enough for her.

'Bless him for that. You know he is the Prime Minister's brother but never acts the big shot, he's always humble. Strict about rules, but humble.'

Viola felt a thud in her chest — she did not expect to hear this and did not know how to react. She had to remain calm and halt the probing questions. Her cheeks were hot as she searched for the right words.

'I would never have guessed that. He is a humble man much like my headmaster in Australia. They are a rare breed in leaders. My take is that if a teacher is hardworking and respectful, then they deserve to be acknowledged. Rank goes in the dust with us.' She knew she had gushed more than she intended. Her father said when she was in a corner, she could sell a car to a successful car salesman.

'I think Mr Alexakis will struggle with letting you go back to Australia. He has had a few, how shall I say... a few thorns that have created problems for him.'

'That happens everywhere when lust for power corrupts

the intended duty.' Viola was on a roll, she witnessed so much across institutions and countries that she could, without a doubt, say that human nature had no borders in that department.

Maria smiled as Viola spoke, 'Your mama and papa must be such proud parents. You are a level-headed young woman.'

She felt Maria's loneliness, a flower reaching for a radiant sunbeam. Viola was what she needed, a kind, caring ear, free of judgement and malice.

When Maria left to complete her morning errands, Viola knew she would want to stay in touch with her when she returned to Sydney. She contemplated Maria's revelation about Miles being the PM's brother. This piece of information was suffocating. Miles would be shocked and angered if he got wind of her vigilante mission. He was not her friend, neither was Jace who left much to be desired as a leader. She trusted that Maria and Vince were the Aurora friends she could count on.

Friday passed as a relaxed, absent headmaster day. A basketball match between staff and students created a buzz. Viola joined in although her skills in the game were a little rusty. She knew her evening with Sebastian would be serious, so she was ready to take on the fun rather than the challenge of the game. Jace Dimakos extended the lunch break to accommodate the match with the shortening of the last lesson to just thirty minutes. He hovered in the background monitoring staff and students in his usual insipid manner. When the match was in full swing, Viola caught sight of the young French teacher manoeuvring her way across to her with a vigorous bouncing of the ball as she edged her way along. When she got close enough, she bumped Viola with her elbow and danced away. A few seconds later she did it again. The third time, Viola spun out of her way and turned to face her. What she heard the young French teacher say sent a shiver through her.

'Beware Ms Bardo, you are being watched!'

Before Viola could ask her what she meant she jogged off the court, throwing the ball to a student. The stunning Claudette Dupont knew something to make such a threat. Viola turned to walk off the court when Vince grabbed her arm.

'You okay, Viola. You look like you've seen a ghost.'

'More like heard one.'

'What do you mean?'

'Nothing, got to run Vince, see you after class.' She looked up into the penetrating eyes of Jace Dimakos. His unsmiling face sent another shiver through her.

VIOLA WAS RELIEVED when the school day was over. Students rushed out leaving equipment strewn on the floor. There was much on her mind and she let them get away without tidying the room. She picked up and stacked the equipment in the cupboards and turned around to find Jace, standing with legs astride at her classroom door.

'Oh, sorry Jace, I didn't realize you were there. Are you after something?' She kicked herself for stating the obvious, and for slipping up with the forbidden first name address. She saw the injured look on his face. Australian bluntness was never intentionally rude. It was an expression to understand what someone wanted, 'are you after something?' left Jace stunned for a few seconds, then he changed the subject.

'Quite a game you had there this afternoon, you seemed to have loads of fun.'

'Yeah it was great to have a bit of fun with the students, I had a good time.'

'Would you join me for dinner tonight in Syntagma Square? I could show you around our brilliant city.'

She had to react fast while thinking about what to say that would not make him feel injured.

'That's kind of you, but I promised to meet a friend for dinner tonight. Perhaps some other time?'

He was quiet for a few seconds, his signature awkwardness returned, he stood upright.

'Next time, have a good evening.' He turned, raised his hand in a goodbye gesture and walked out the door.

Viola expected nothing else. He was gushing when they first met, then the flowers, now a dinner invitation — that had to be crossing all the headmaster's strict rules for staff and students.

She called a cab and, on the drive to meet Sebastian, all she could think about was Claudette's warning but soon forgot Jace's strangeness.

He was who he was.

8

Sebastian waited outside the pizzeria. They decided to try the place again for the gastronomical delight they enjoyed the other night. He was not his dapper self — creased shirt, unshaven, red-nosed, and bleary-eyed. Viola wondered if he had been drinking, or had a difficult day.

'Hi Sebastian,' she was careful not to step on his toes by asking how he was. He coughed and explained that he was not feeling well and perhaps coming down with the flu. *Coming down*, he had it already and was likely to pass it on to her! He coughed into his elbow, not like some who coughed and sneezed with no sense of social responsibility. Here now was a decent man, a gentleman. She liked that.

It was a warm night. The air clung in a tight, moist sleeve around her. She had hoped for a long stroll after a decadent pizza dinner, but Sebastian was in no state for a stroll anywhere, and it would be unfair to expect him to do that. His stooped shoulders were a clear indication that he was in the grip of man flu and it would only get worse by the time she was ready to head back to Aurora for the night. She knew she should not heap any sympathy upon him as that would make him a child and her his mother! The only thing to do was to suggest what might well compromise her health.

'If it helps you relax, we can go back to your apartment. I could get the pizza and meet you there.'

Sebastian coughed again and pulled his cardigan across his chest — dear god he must have a fever if he thinks it's cold on this warm evening. He insisted on waiting outside while she ordered the pizza. Ten minutes later she stepped out onto the street. He was gone! After a hurried look behind the pizza shop, she rang him when she had no reply to her text message.

'I'm sorry Viola,' he groaned, 'I did not mean to scare you, I thought you would have figured out that I returned to the apartment.'

She was annoyed, but let it go. He was unwell after all. Armed with two-and-a-half pizzas she walked to his apartment. It was a five-minute walk. She picked up her pace when she heard a familiar voice call out from across the street and approach her.

'Casual dining tonight, Ms Bardo?'

Jace Dimakos walked up to her with no smile and raised his left hand in greeting. Claudette Dupont clung to his right arm! She hung on so tight as if a gale force wind was threatening to yank them apart!

Viola heard her own voice echo from deep inside.

'Oh, hello... my friend is unwell, so we are supping at home tonight on fast food. Easiest option under the circumstances.'

Jace grinned as if he had caught her lying.

'Have a good evening, Ms Bardo.' He sauntered away before she could say anything more. She cringed knowing that he reveled in noticing her discomfit in seeing him, with Claudette to boot! He would think she fobbed off his dinner invitation for a nothing evening. While this was humiliating, it was best that he had no idea who she was meeting. He was her assistant headmaster and her host and now she appeared to be an impostor — all respect that he might have had for her, gone! She accepted the small mercy of being alone or Jace would have thought that Sebastian was her beau! He could have Claudette — now her warning made sense! She reminded herself that she was on a mission to serve Tempest to find the child and have him sent back to his father. Seven days was all they had.

A sniveling Sebastian opened the apartment door for her looking worse than when she left him. He noticed her glum face.

'I'm really sorry for not letting you know I headed back here, please forgive me. I felt queasy and had to leave.'

'No problem, I'm not upset with you. I bumped into Jace Dimakos, Aurora's assistant headmaster, while I was rushing up the street with the pizza! Can you imagine?'

'You poor thing, ruined your image?' Sebastian managed a smile.

She hated that he was enjoying her momentary fall from grace, something a devilish younger brother would relish, but she overlooked it.

Her mother warned her about this side of her personality, telling her not to be a doormat to others.

An hour later Sebastian was brighter with a pizza and ginger brandy in his belly. He was ready to tell her about his findings.

'Matthew Soto dropped the boy off at your school around 8:40 this morning. He stopped at the coffee shop at the end of the street and I followed him in but sat a safe distance away to avoid suspicion or detection that he was being followed. Soto spoke to someone on his cell phone, but I could not hear the gist of that conversation from where I sat, or he might have been whispering.'

Viola's knitted brow told him he was in for some criticism.

'That was way too dangerous being close to him in a confined space. You cannot risk being identified. You know the rules Sebastian, and let us not forget he is ex-military!'

'I left after Soto departed, and I assure you, he did not once look in my direction. I drove over to the PM's house and parked behind the football field across from his house and observed him picking up a woman. She might be the PM's wife. Then I drove to Soto's house knowing that he was out on an errand. I got out the car and walked towards the house.'

Viola's jaw dropped, 'You didn't! Please tell me you did not go to the house.'

'I did under the pretext of being lost and needing directions. Nobody answered the door, but I saw a child peer out the window and a woman inside pulled him away. I noticed a few strewn toys in the garden so it's not my imagination that there's a child in the house.'

Her load was eased with him doing all the field work while she did her research from inside the school and used a psychological angle to garner information.

'We have to get inside the house somehow to confirm if this is indeed the child or if there are other children in the house. This will involve you going in.'

Viola sucked in her breath and felt her hand creep to her shirt pocket for a piece of brittle wrapped in crinkled foil. She detested being told what to do. She ran her own operation in other parts of the world — now Tempest saddled her with Sebastian, a nice guy, but at times an annoying one!

'So, what will you have me do? Should I take notes or is it simple enough to comprehend?'

'Something has played right into our hands so it's simple.'

Viola sat on the edge of her seat not wanting to miss a thing.

'Soto or someone associated with him placed an advertisement for a nanny or governess in the local paper. I called for the location. It's Soto's place!'

'Good work, 99!' Viola laughed, 'Am I to apply for the position?' Admiration returned, he took risks, but he delivered.

'Just to get in for an interview. Fingers crossed he will conduct it at the house so that you can do some unobtrusive sleuthing.'

'I can't take on another position, how will that work?'

'It's impossible for you to take on another role, but a curious look in is all we need.'

SEBASTIAN EXPLAINED that he thought the woman in the house with the child might be Soto's mother. She appeared older. A call to Tempest on the latest development was necessary.

Her deep, husky voice crooned on the other end of the line.

'Good evening both! How are we? I'm satisfied at this stage with the developments and decisions. Getting closer to Soto by getting inside the house, if possible, is an excellent idea. Good work Sebastian, on spying the advertisement for a nanny. Chat later.' She wafted off into space without a goodbye or waiting to hear their response.

Viola shot a look of shock, surprise, and a tinge of horror in Sebastian's direction.

'How on earth did she know all that? Did you speak to her earlier?'

Sebastian rolled his eyes, 'She's listening in most of the time now. There's a chip in both our cell phones. No privacy unless your phone is not on your person or nearby.'

On that note Tempest breezed back on the line.

'Sorry Viola, I need up-to-date, in-the-minute information in this delicate situation with a clock ticking faster than we can think.'

'I understand,' a subdued Viola said.

'I have you booked with a dentist, a Dr Horatio. You must get to him by four, tomorrow afternoon. He's based at the

Athena General Hospital. Cut out the peanut brittle if you want good teeth at my age.'

Viola's cheeks burned with embarrassment. She felt she was a child being chastised by her mother even though Tempest was gentle.

'Thank you Tempest, I will go to that appointment.'

'One more thing before I flit off, some information I raked up. Soto had counseling after his hip injury to cope with his aggression.'

'How aggressive was he?' Sebastian asked.

'Go figure, he's ex-military, so I assume, he is armed and dangerous. He's been quiet in Athens since his arrival. Nothing seems to have triggered any outbursts. Now turn off the listening mode, I need to get some rest. Sleep well.'

Viola dashed for her phone checking the settings for where she could turn off Tempest's active listening.

'You can't turn it off, I have access to the chip control and can disable all devices connected. I've turned it off. Relax. Look at you, you're a mess!'

'I am uncomfortable about things I cannot control.'

'Dear God, Viola, you will have a stroke if you don't chill sometimes. Hey each to his own!' He laughed, looking at her with a cheeky sidewards glance.

'We don't speak ill of Tempest, there has been no reason to, but can you imagine if we did. I would end up on tranquilizers if that was the case and lose all control then!'

'You're too good for your own good.'

'What's that supposed to mean?'

'You seem so clean.'

'I don't know what you mean, don't make assumptions about me this early. You might be disappointed. How long have you known about the chip?'

'Just today, I intended to let you know, but we were rushed and wanted the case updates first.'

She looked at him with disbelief, thinking he wanted to see her squirm. He told her it was not downloadable software, but a chip Tempest had devised to communicate without detection.

'You should insert the chip control into your phone so you can deactivate it whenever you choose to, or activate it when you need assistance. Tempest can intervene to help out. It has its benefit, a huge benefit. She has given us two chips with controls.'

When he said it like that, she had to agree that it was worth having it in her phone.

'There are wrist watches too that we can activate. They act like two-way radios. Quite James *Bondish*.'

He handed her a black leather wristwatch. She shoved it into the side pocket of her handbag, wished him a hurried goodnight and left. Sebastian invited her to stay over on a Friday night but she had to maintain some distance and had the awkward vision of seeing him come out the shower with a bare chest and dangling towel around his waist. That would not happen! Her aunt Lorenza drilled being circumspect around men. She believed that women had to protect themselves by reserving their dignity for themselves. A measure of distance was a good thing she said. Viola could hear her voice and see her earnest expression in those life lessons that matured her at nine, far earlier than her mother liked. Viola absorbed her aunt's words like spiritual lessons. Where her mother erred, Lorenza was a comforting presence in her young life. But Lorenza, young as she was, ensured she maintained being an aunt without Viola expecting that she would bend her rules as friends would. Viola ached to see her again to know she was alive, and well, and might someday return. Her father craved closure. The need to settle grief is an unending palpable yearning

Viola left Sebastian around midnight. She was desperate for a good night's sleep to have a clear head for the quick thinking needed to get through all they had planned. The clock was ticking too fast. Her cab driver was an unfriendly man, a nod and grunt, was all she got. What followed within a matter of seconds after the driver set off for Aurora was an unexpected hellish experience.

Blinding lights behind her and the driver's raised voice, 'What the hell is this guy doing! Hang on Miss!' sent her heart spinning. The driver swerved to the left lane and darted back to the right, screeching tires and the smell of rubber made her queasy. The driver yelled, 'Are you being followed?'

Viola clung to the seat in front of her, 'No! I don't know what's going on!'

As the driver took another swerve to the left lane, she turned to see who was in the vehicle creating the commotion. A glint of streetlight illuminated the right side of the car.

She gasped — the vehicle was a dark Mercedes with a lone driver!

9

I t was time to make that call to her mother.

She had put it off long enough. A strong cup of coffee and a piece of peanut brittle would fortify her for what was to come. Negativity was not Viola's way, but sometimes things stayed as they were and accepting that, prevented bitterness from creeping into their relationship. With the creamy caramel taste cascading in her mouth with bits of peanut teasing her palate she wondered at what age this addiction began.

HER MOTHER SOUNDED cheerful and eager to chat. She detested Viola's sleep-ins during her school holidays — her trumpet wake-up call was the repetitive melodious singing of *carpe diem,* until she got a response from her daughter.

Motherhood was a title to her. She treated the role like a job. Strict emotionless rules applied with no negotiations into her decisions. Viola contemplated what her mother was like as a teacher and head of her faculty — did she treat her adult students with the same coldness? Her parent's arguments were dominant memories with her father sighing, 'Helena, let it go please, not in front of Artista, please,' but Helena had to win the argument before she would back down. With her mother, it was best to agree on everything she said and ladle oodles of praise on how good she was at all she did. Her mother was always mother, never mom or mama.

'Good morning mother, how have you been?'

'Ah Viola, good morning, it has been a long time. Why so long? I am well and you?'

Viola wriggled in her seat, waiting for the next question — 'are you eating and exercising?'

'Yes, I am well and taking good care of myself and my work here in Athens.' Her mother equated a life worthless without a grinding exercise regime before breakfast three hundred and sixty-five days of the year. And the quarter in three hundred and sixty-five and a quarter, went to cooking Christmas lunch with a 5 am start while most households slept in after the revelry of Christmas Eve. Her father remained locked in for days in the grip of creative mania and this sadly earned him her mother's title of a 'waste of a man.'

'That's good, how is your father? You speak to him every day, right?'

'Not every day when I'm on an exchange mission but twice a week when I'm back in Australia.' She bit her lip needing to defend her closeness to her father. 'He's asked me to spend Christmas with him. I think he's lonely.'

Dead silence on the other end made Viola regret that she had spoken more than she should have. She braced herself for what would follow.

'That's his choice, nobody told him to be lonely or that to *live* is not his right!'

It was time to turn the conversation around to avoid the childhood repetitions that assaulted her ears.

'How's Jonah and the dancing lessons?'

'He's good, exceptionally good. We will be in Spain in six months entering a dancing competition. It's on Jonah's bucket list.'

Viola's ears burned, she was happy for her mother and her husband but what annoyed her was the change in how her mother bent to all Jonah wanted. She enrolled in dancing classes to ensure she was on par with his skills. As a mathematics professor and head of the literature faculty, they could afford a sprawling mansion in Clifton Beach and an apartment in central Cape Town. Then another question that Viola knew was coming somewhere in their conversation.

'Met any handsome young men lately? You're getting on, now, soon childbearing years will be over.' Why would her mother talk about the child-bearing years when she had zero maternal qualities?

'Work keeps me busy and I like it that way. Just like you do,' it was difficult to keep up being pleasant with mother, 'what's the latest at the university?' There, she did it at the right moment, by opening the door, away from further questions about her personal life! Now Helena had the floor, Viola was safe!

'My research has paid off. The university will publish my book early in February next year. Upon hearing each new bit of news on her mother's achievements, she interjected with marvelous and how wonderful. Then, much to her relief came her mother's welcome end to the conversation!

HER THOUGHTS TURNED to how she could engage the Prime Minister's son to help advance the safe return of the abducted child to his father in Germany. She had to finish all she had to do by three that afternoon to get to the dentist on time. A gnawing ache in her mouth shifted from the right side to the left. She popped a clove onto the chipped tooth and bit down. The relief was instantaneous! Good old home remedies were the best for quick relief from a nasty toothache.

For some respite in her afternoon lesson, she would ask students to share something new or special in their lives, a way for her to get the PM's son talking about his family.

That afternoon, year nine gathered outside her classroom, eager for her laid-back atmosphere and fun activities. It excited them when she announced what she was doing. Students separated into groups of four to five and the chatter began. It was hard to keep the volume down when learning was taking place. Within five minutes hands flew up to share what the group had discussed. The PM's son held the attention of his group of four with his vigorous hand actions. Viola walked across to the group.

'What do we have here, Mr Sanchez, you either tell a good story or have some exciting news to share? Come and share it by stepping to the front of the room.'

'That's awesome, thanks Ms Bardo, but may I speak from here.'

'Yes, go ahead,' Viola wondered whether Brendan Sanchez was nervous or just wanted his way. He was a nice enough kid, quiet and lacking the impulsiveness of boys his age, but he was not easy to figure out as she assumed.

'Attention class, Brendan has something interesting to share, stop and turn to face him.'

The lad cleared his throat, and his eyes shone with pride, 'I've been doing some private tutoring, how's that! And I am enjoying it because I am also learning a bit of German too during these sessions.'

Hands shot up with eager questions desperate for answers. One student yelled from the back of the room.

'What's that then, are you involved with the Nazi's?'

'That is an unnecessary remark,' Viola said in a tone and look to freeze hell over.

The boy held up his hands in prayerful forgiveness, 'I'm sorry Ms Bardo, I did not mean that at all.'

Viola was calm and easy-going, but her students knew when enough was enough, her look made wayward boys quiver in their boots. She earned respect for her nurturing, generous nature and to lose that scared the life out of some.

'One question at a time, but let's hear Brendan tell us his story first then we shall commence with questions from the back left corner of the classroom.

'Thank you, Ms Bardo. Well, here's how it all began,' Viola listened with a serious face to the drama Brendan was creating, 'a family friend has a nephew from Germany who needs help learning English so I've been helping out some days after school and the kid helps me with understanding some basic everyday German words.'

One persistent hand caught Viola's attention, and she allowed the question.

'How can a kid teach you much German with their limited English?'

'Good question,' Viola applauded.

'I follow up with YouTube lessons to merge what I want to learn quickly but because the kid has limited English, sign language helps me get around what he says. The joy I see in the kid when he understands something has made me feel like I want to be a teacher.' Brendan looked at Viola for acknowledgement.

'Teaching is a noble profession and you are right, the joy in shifting understanding and improving learning is the reward of teaching. Who knows, you may one day be headmaster at Aurora?'

'Mr Alexakis won't be happy about that Ms Bardo,' one student piped in from the front of the room. The class laughed and Viola ignored the remark.

She noticed a shadow hovering close to her door and knew it was Jace snooping around because of the buzz from her room. Her philosophy was that a silent classroom was a classroom where no learning was happening. There was a time for both — silence in exam rooms, not her classroom!

* * *

VIOLA ARRIVED at the dentist right on time and was surprised to find that he was an Australian. She was not expecting to meet a fellow countryman. He had married a Greek woman who was studying in Queensland where they met as university students. They married as soon as they graduated, and he moved to Athens. For his fifteen years as an Athenian, he was as Aussie as Viola's neighbors in Sydney. With the history settled and between her 'hmmm' and 'ah' responses he showed an interest that she was teaching at Aurora Academy. Soon the conversation drifted to speculations on Miles Alexakis.

'Your headmaster is an interesting bloke. The silent type for someone in his line of work. He's good at his job but a dark horse if ever I saw one.' He raised a questioning eyebrow.

Viola responded with 'hmmm' and raised her palm to show she did not understand what Dr Horatio meant. This opened the floodgate to secrets and strange occurrences that Viola was dubious to accept as the truth on Miles.

'It's no secret that he's the Prime Minister's brother. One wonders whether that's how he's in that position as head of Aurora. It has baffled locals. That the school is not lacking in funds also adds to suspicions on whether they receive more compared to other schools in the region. The dentist nodded after each comment confirming he wanted Viola to accept his views. She wanted him to stop. Miles was not the reason she was in Athens and his history had no bearing on what she had to do. But he continued, having his patients tongue-tied by his activities, gave him full rein to say whatever he wanted.

'There's been dissatisfaction that staff were underpaid but the upper crust like Alexakis and that side-kick assistant of his are on the gravy train. It won't surprise me if they are.'

Viola was relieved when her filling was done, she rinsed out her mouth with the dental assistant's knowing look that there was too much chit-chat going on. She was ready to say thank you and leave when Dr Horatio's jaw was at work again.

'Did you know that Miles Alexakis is married, but nobody sees the wife these days?'

'No, I don't have any information on his private life.' She was itching to say that she was not interested but remembered that Tempest had made this booking for her and she would have to tolerate the dentist's wagging tongue. In her line of justice work, wagging tongues brought important clues to the investigation, but petty gossip infuriated her. It was bad enough that Jace Dimakos had cooled off her. She did not need Miles thinking she was gossiping about him with locals.

'They have been together for twelve years but in recent years doctors diagnosed her with bipolar disorder. She's rarely out in public. He must have her locked away in the attic.' Viola was unsure if he was joking as his serious face gave nothing away.

'Your teeth are not in a healthy state, Ms Bardo. You need to see me again in two weeks.'

Her teeth needed intense work. Dr Horatio did not tell her anything new. All she needed was to know was how to stop the advancing deterioration.

'I will book in a day with your receptionist. Thank you.'

She was glad to hear the sound of traffic out on the street. It was strangely soothing.

A CALL from Sebastian confirmed a morning meeting in an interesting location.

She needed an early night.

10

Sebastian waited for Viola at the changing of the guard. A large crowd had gathered in readiness to witness this ceremonial change over.

Sebastian waltzed towards Viola and kissed her on both cheeks. She flushed a few shades darker when he whispered in her ear. 'We call this keeping up appearances as a couple like many others here, today.' He squeezed her shoulder showing no response was necessary. She put her arm around his waist in response and leaned her head on his shoulder. The natural way she slipped into his game plan chuffed him. This made them good at what they did. Keeping up appearances was a necessary step.

Under her breath she said, 'I hope this is in the spirit of what we have to achieve.'

He whispered with rehearsed adoration in his eyes, 'That is all it is.'

Okay she thought, I deserved that, but work is work.

THE DOMESTIC DISCORD of her childhood in overhearing arguments between her parents left its indelible memory. She was cautious in avoiding commitment. This was her choice, her innate fear of having the same life her parents endured before they divorced. She lost many wonderful opportunities with young men who wanted a commitment but she was never ready and could never say if she would ever be ready to take that step with her work demands in recent years. A yearning for closeness with that one special person who would know her in the way she needed, lingered beneath the surface, unresolved. To expect anyone to ignore what her work involved and have her lack of long-term commitment was too much to ask any civilized, starry-eyed young man. Sebastian gave her a lesson on what keeping up appearances in relationships entailed. Her parents tried to be civil to each other in public and professional circles but behind closed doors the knives were out. Two passionate artists who could never be Dali and Gala.

She observed the families, couples and friends hugging each other in expectation of the spectacle, the drama of the changing of the guard at Parliament House. Each faced their own wars, taking a holiday, hoping to mend the tattered state of their lives, or perhaps they were blessed with bliss. The poetic muse surged, she committed to memory what she hoped to recall in a quiet space, away from the jostling crowd. Now she observed human behavior in all its honesty and deception. A middle-aged man kissed the top of his wife's head — her stony, sullen face hid no truths.

She broke into Sebastian's reverie.

'I have information that Miles Alexakis is the Prime Minister's brother.' No response. She could not believe he ignored her comment, staring ahead, deep in thought. She threw in that the dentist flowed like the Edessa waterfalls. Still no response. His eyes remained fixed on the crowd.

Then he nudged her and whispered with his lips close to

her ear, 'Look left in the far corner. See the woman with the blue dress, she's holding the child's hand and the man next to her?' She felt his hot breath blow down her ear — his agitation dissolved his keeping up of appearances.

Realization dawned.

'Yes, he has a walking stick... is that...' Before she could utter his name, Sebastian nodded and squeezed her arm again.

'Dear God, he must not catch sight of our faces, we have to slip further back into the crowd.'

'Just look straight ahead at the guards, we can use peripheral vision to observe his movements.'

She had difficulty remaining still in tense moments, now she forced herself to look ahead, it was easier for her to lean up against Sebastian to stop her twitching movements while keeping up the appearance of being a loving couple. She had to engage in small talk.

'Have you noticed the guards are all the same height? Do you think it's deliberate?'

'Perhaps. See how revered the unknown soldier is with his tomb at the centre. This is a short changeover. We should head across to the flea market to talk at ease once this is over.'

The changing of the guard was complete, and it was time for photographs — Viola noted that Matthew Soto picked up the boy and walked away from the crowd with the woman, a much older person, following behind him at a slower pace. Soon they disappeared from sight.

'We cannot follow them. It will be obvious that we are as the crowd away from here is sparse. My concern is that Soto must not recognize you. Did you get a response for the nanny application?'

'I prefer *au pair*, but no, it has only been twenty-four hours since I emailed my application.'

'Yes, the reason you need to remain a stranger to him, don't give him any memories to recall. Remember, the military trained him to observe, recognize and recall. These skills are heightened, almost an animal instinct.'

'I don't know, I somehow sense that Soto is a caring uncle. The boy was clinging to him. Did you see how he rested his head on Soto's shoulder when he picked him up?'

'Who knows? The innocence of babes to perceptions of kindness. We must not drop our guard with him. If he has taken a child without parental consent, then he is a ruthless person.'

Viola looked at Sebastian with curiosity riddled eyes — what was it that made him react this way?

'I agree about not dropping our guard around him, but we must have a balanced view into the situation if we are to serve due justice on the matter.'

'Absolutely! Nothing less will do.'

For all his good intentions, she would act on her own instincts — it had served her well in the past.

They strolled over to the flea market. Soto and the child, with the woman standing behind them, were at the fruit stand.

'Slow down,' Sebastian hissed, 'we have to turn around to keep out of his sight.'

'Wow, those bananas look amazing, I hope we can return to get some.' She heard him click something onto his sunglasses. 'What was that?'

'Rear view lens. With this I can observe where the three are.'

Viola was never one for new-fangled technology, it amazed her how equipped Sebastian was. It had to be a gift from Tempest.

'They're walking away. Seems like an innocent family day out. I had visions of the boy being locked away in a room.'

'It would take a monster to do something like that. Your Richard III, locking his nephews in the Tower of London, just awful.'

'Don't go soft on Soto now. I like the analogy. You've picked up on my pet high school peeve!' Sebastian's reckless laugh was refreshing. It was the first time she was in company with a person outside of teaching who shared her *Shakespearean-isms.*

'I need some of those bananas, I'll be back in a split second.' Before he could stop her, she sprinted to the fruit stall. His heart skipped a beat when he saw the woman walking in the direction of the fruit stalls. Viola might walk right into her and blow her cover. He did a three hundred and sixty degree turn to see if Soto had returned to the vicinity, not trusting his rear-view device. No sign of him and Viola was back with a large bag of bananas, wolfing one down!

'Phew, that was a narrow escape. Did you even realize that you pushed past the woman at the fruit stand?'

'What woman? Soto's?'

'You fixated on getting those bananas that you did not see her. So where are you hiding your troupe of monkeys with all these bananas?'

'I haven't seen such lovely bananas in a long time, although we get prime stock from Queensland. I won't call Vince and Maria a troupe of monkeys but kind people around me.' Her nose in the air on that note made Sebastian double up with laughter again. 'You say that like a devoted wife!'

'Stop this mirth, everything I do seems to make you laugh, we have serious business to attend to now. Get this straight I won't be such a wife to anyone!'

'I'm messing around, don't get offended.'

Viola dropped her stiff attitude with a brief shrug. There was too much to observe for sensitivities to get in the way.

* * *

BACK AT SEBASTIAN'S APARTMENT, a call to Tempest had her

hanging onto every word when they revealed the events of their day.

'Up close and personal, almost! Not good, just yet, I declare.'

'We were careful as Viola has to meet Soto face-to-face for the interview, which I'm sure will happen soon.' Sebastian added.

'Have you worked out how you will ask for time out of your teaching to moonlight as Soto's governess when granted an interview and accepted.'

'I imagine I will need at least three days and tenatively notified the school when I arrived that I would apply for some days out. The dates were left open until the need arose.'

'By the way, the German Ambassador is due in Greece in three days to attend the climate summit in Athens. You both need to move faster now — you're down to six days, remember.'

Tempest clicked off before they could pose any questions.

'Let's hope we can clear everything so that the German Ambassador can return home with his son.'

Sebastian explained that he would find a way to get into Soto's house even if he had to go incognito as a door-to-door salesman of educational toys and books for pre-school-aged children. Viola accepted his plan although she had reservations about whether the woman would invite him into house.

IN THE GARDEN AT AURORA, Vince was pottering around the little strip in front of his cottage. He waved a gloved hand at her.

'Hey Viola! I thought you were out for the weekend.'

'I had some work to finish here, so I had to get back. I will go out again later, how about you? What love are you putting into the ground?'

He laughed, 'Fresh basil to garnish my food, and I place them in little vases around the house. It works wonders for the mood with the uplifting fragrance.'

Viola admired his earth-child spirit, so much like her father until he went on a wine binge and defended it as a plant-based drink! She wished she could be as carefree as Vince, but knew her life was only free when she served the needy and desperate and achieved justice for them.

'I have a pot of fresh green tea brewing, care to come over for a cup?'

'Finish your gardening, I'll pop over later for a quick cuppa when I finish what I have to do.'

SHE KICKED OFF HER SHOES, put on an oversized shirt and jumped onto the couch with her laptop. In her email spam folder, sat an email from Matthew Soto. He wanted to interview her! She replied that she accepted the interview.

She froze when Soto replied in an instant, confirming a meeting at the Oceans Conference Centre.

The formal venue puzzled her. It was an interview for an au pair position.

She was eager to get into his home soon.

11

Viola attended a multitude of interviews as an exchange teacher, in Australia, on-line, and in person outside Australia. Yet now she tossed and turned, unsure how she should present at Matthew Soto's interview. She had to meet the child but had to get the man in her corner first. It felt like starting a love affair with a mysterious stranger. Danger was never far off in such situations and there was the undeniable thrill in saving a life. She responded to the advertisement in a legitimate newspaper so what harm could befall her? Regardless of her vigilante justice life these questions popped up when stress rankled to validate her ordinary, sensitive side. What should she wear? What should she say? Her cell phone pinged on her bedside table. A message from her father, short, simple, and timely, 'Love you Artista!' This calmed her, she rolled over and shut her eyes in search of a few hours of trouble-free sleep.

AN EARLY MORNING message from Sebastian suggested they take an official tour of Parliament House. She thought it unnecessary as the Prime Minister was not under investigation, not theirs anyway, and if she was meeting Matthew Soto face-to-face such an excursion would be a waste of valuable time. Days were limited and answers were far and few. The clock was now a gentle gong heightening the urgency to get the case moving for the child's safety.

JUST WHEN SHE thought she had her head around most things an email arrived announcing a staff meeting before the start of the school day. She had to call Vince to find out why there was this short notice. He was her information bureau in the tight-lipped Aurora community. Maria had slipped out of her thoughts these past few days with much happening both in her head and her physical world. Meeting Matthew Soto alone that afternoon loomed when her rational mind questioned whether she should ask Sebastian for back-up. She reminded herself that she was a lone worker, enjoying solitude to figure out the best direction to take when she was on a case.

A GRAVE-FACED Miles Alexakis sat at the head of a rather long table in a small, tight room. Insufferable, once sweet, Jace Dimakos stood rigid and purse-lipped behind him, subservient as always. Miles tapped his coffee cup with his teaspoon to call the room to order. Today placid staff were out of character, agitated and chatty — on tenterhooks about the sudden morning meeting before a busy day.

'Good morning, I apologize for this sudden interruption to your day. A situation has arisen that affects us as a community and some teachers specifically.' A few throats cleared as everybody fixed a worried look at Miles, unsure whether this was leading to more duties secretly waiting to pounce on them. 'I've been on the telephone with police this morning.' A few deep sighs passed across the room as the worst was expected. Had somebody died?

Jace's intense look made her skin crawl — had he discovered her dual role, and would he name and shame her? Hell, Miles, out with it! Her head hammered.

'One of our students is missing since this morning as reported by the parents. They saw their child at dinner last night when nothing seemed untoward.'

Now a soft ripple of sighs and a few groans were audible enough for Miles to call the room to order. He played the irate judge with ease. No questions asked, and Viola felt the desperation to know more. Why the secrecy on the student's name and gender? She raised her hand like an impulsive student who had not given the question, she was eager to ask, due attention. Miles looked at her and pretended not see her stiff, upright arm.

Nothing would stop her.

'Mr Alexakis, who is the missing student?'

From a sigh and groan — silence swallowed the room. Viola had taken a bold and brazen step among the complacent and passive. Here she was, the newbie, and an exchange teacher to boot, demanding an answer. She thought she was being polite in asking a most reasonable question. This time Miles cleared his throat.

'This is a delicate matter, Ms Bardo, so we ensure that we protect the student and his family at all times.'

Hallelujah!

Finally!

He reveals gender!

Then Miles issued a cultish command.

'Please raise your hands if you accept that privacy is mandatory to protect the family from the media and harsh social criticism.'

Her dropped jaw did not go unnoticed by Jace, amid the unified low whispered 'aye!' This was a live parliamentary session with headless chooks in attendance!

'There is a document at the entrance for you to sign that you agree to the privacy around this situation. I repeat the student's safety is paramount. Do you have any objections to signing this document?'

What an idiot to think that anybody would object in an open threatening forum. Silence was what he wanted and what he got.

'Any objections?' he asked again, this time in a louder voice and with a scowling face.

Passive aggressiveness, bullying dressed in good clothes, something she knew well, she heard her own disgruntled breathing in the silence of her female peers. A noose tightened around all their necks as they sat in what appeared to be a criminal tribunal for something they hadn't committed or had any inkling about.

Then the revelation, 'The student in question is Brendon Sanchez.'

Vince looked across the table at Viola. Her blood chilled, dear god he thinks I have something to do with this because I showed an interest in wanting to know more about the kid.

Miles continued, 'He is an outstanding, respectful student and we owe it to our school to protect him by giving our allegiance to his family.'

Yeah right, he is your nephew so how much more do you want from the staff? Now Viola was choking on her silence, the voice in her head demanded that the hypocrisy stop.

'Do not on any account speak to the media. If you do, consider it a dismissible offense.'

Dr Horatio's revelations had a familiar ring now.

The uncontrollable twitch in her neck had to be stopped, or

Dimakos was at the ever ready to make her believe she was guilty. Now Vince would want to speak to her!

A scurrying to the back of the room had teachers signing the secrecy clause with Miles and Jace watching on, brothers in arms. Much to Viola's surprise, Claudette Dupont was controlling the signing of the document — a peacock, fanning her plume in the glory of a fake position — in with the family!

THE SCHOOL DAY passed with tension brewing among teachers who wanted to talk but Miles ensured their lips were locked. On the bus to the Oceans Conference Room she pondered whether all students, unrelated to Miles, would get the same treatment. There was a lot going on at Aurora and the dentist's words continued to echo in favor of his criticisms of the institution. If he had really dropped some truths, what else lay hidden in the dark corners of Miles Alexakis' mind?

A few men in black suits entered and left Miles' office during the day. An unprecedented shutting of the school for a day would attract media attention with his connection to Parliament House. Viola had to keep calm for her interview that afternoon.

* * *

AT THE OCEANS MEETING ROOM, a young woman approached Viola asking if she was Ms Bardo. The woman told her that Mr Soto was waiting for her in the oval room. A stomach gyration is a terrifying thing when in a strange place with no known access to amenities for the call of nature. Her clammy palms dripped onto the handbag she clutched to her chest. She paused, inhaled deeply, raised her head a notch and walked to the oval room. The door was ajar, with a gentle prod it opened.

The back of a man's graying head greeted her. He was

looking out at the ocean through the bay windows. Shadowy Erebus not ready to reveal his face. She heard a gentle, deep voice.

'Good afternoon, Ms Bardo. Thank you for being prompt. I detest tardiness,' she heard him sigh. 'Biscuits and coffee are at the back to your right. Grab a cup and make yourself comfortable at the table.'

'Thank you,' she whispered in child-like docility. She noted that his left hand clutched a large brass knob fixed to a wooden stick. He leaned forward to secure himself to a standing position. If ever she needed a piece of peanut brittle, it was now, the crunch in her mouth would break the razor tense air between them. The cranked-up air conditioner sent a shiver through her. She had to get inside his head to understand his mysterious aura.

Matthew Soto moved with a deliberate dragging gait to the head of the conference table making no eye contact with her. Once seated across from her he slowly raised his eyes. She saw the deepest blue eyes set in an intricate mapped face. He seemed older than the voice that greeted her. He nodded but made no attempt to come across to shake her hand as was customary in formal introductions. Instead, there was a spark of warmth in his oceanic blue eyes. That put her at ease, her chilled palms were no longer sweaty and the mambo in her belly settled to a slow waltz.

'Punctuality is a priority for me.'

He ensured she understood that. If only he knew how obsessive this schoolteacher was about time. His military life made time crucial. He would get to the point, she knew, with no fluff. All he would want to know is if she could deliver what he needed.

'Ms Bardo tell me a bit about yourself, I know you are Australian and an au pair seeking work. Your credentials are impressive, the best candidate in the batch I received. Tell me why Greece and not anywhere else in the world?'

'Thank you, Mr Soto,' she said with a slight incline of the head. Her father maintained that humility went a long way in life while pride and ego choked on the vile froth of self-importance setting one up for a hellish existence. 'Greece has always fascinated me with its rich culture and as the seat of democracy. I courted the idea of a work stint here or moving over for a permanent change of lifestyle.' She wanted to add in details, that the cuisine and sights attracted her, but dropped that. Mr Soto did not seem a man who would engage in trivial talk.

'Good, I see. Why the interest in working with children?'

She explained that she was an only child of divorced parents and she knew first-hand how important it was to feel loved and nurtured.

Matthew Soto studied her face with an unflinching gaze throughout her explanations. She knew he was looking for telltale signs of weakness, reading into her every word — that is the strategy he used in making decisions that affected the lives of others.

'You live in the city so getting to the place I need you to be at is close enough for you.'

She felt a momentary pang of guilt for using Sebastian's address and then horror pinned her to her seat. Had he checked out the street, and perhaps the building, did he see Sebastian leave or arrive at the apartment?

'It's a four-week contract to begin with and the possibility of an extension if things work out. How does that sound to you?'

'That will depend on my work permit and what the conditions of work entail.'

He raised his head an inch higher when he heard her speak of conditions of work. She continued that she was picky about the work she took on and did not blindly walk into any job. Once the words were out she knew that she might have blown the chance of securing the position. Tempest counted on her and now she was unsure of her position.

Then she heard him say, 'Fair enough,' as he steadied himself to stand up, this time to shake her hand and bid her adieu. He promised to have a decision within twenty-four hours should she be the successful candidate. If she was, she had to be available to meet the child before accepting his contract. They parted on amicable professional terms — deep down she knew she might have offended him, but he was a hard one to read, and she was no pushover.

Either way she would know in twenty-four hours.

Passion and uncertainty collided in another mental poem.

Black and white
And quite contrite
Is Soto's motto

SHE STROLLED DOWN SYNTAGMA SQUARE, unable to control a rising giggle, enjoying the secret pleasure of writing a mind poem cuss. Ah the indulgent pleasure of unshared poetry!

There was much to tell Sebastian, she had to process it all first. She took a deviation to extend her mindful pondering.

WHILE SHE WAS in the interview with Soto, Sebastian went to his house as a door-to-door educational toys and books salesperson.

He dashed down to meet her at the fountain around 6 pm, bursting to tell her about his encounter with the woman who came to the door.

'It's like trying to enter Fort Knox, I tell you! She would not budge an inch. How was your day?'

'Meeting Soto was interesting, but the rest was an average day,' she lied. She did not intend telling him yet about her early morning staff meeting.

'Soto got home early today, I could have got caught talking to the woman, he was that early. Seems he did not do the school pick-up run today.' Now she was in a corner and would have to tell him what transpired at Aurora.

Sebastian pushed for answers, 'Was the PM's son at school today?'

'I'll fill you in on what I know soon. Tell me about your book selling expedition.' She needed some time to think, her head was in a scramble. Unlike Sebastian, she did not spout like a burst pipe with new information. She picked her words and moment with care.

Sebastian said, as she predicted, that he was not invited into the house. He stood on the verandah and thought he heard a kiddie's cartoon playing behind the shut entrance hall door. He heard music and shrill voices. A child's laughter was distinct.

The woman fobbed him off saying the boss was away and she could purchase nothing without his permission. She asked for a business card which he could not produce. Then she slammed the door on him.

'There's no way I can try that again, she thinks I'm a fraudster.'

'Well, I suppose we are, in a way.'

1 2

Viola got the call — Soto wanted her to meet the boy. She was going into the den at 4:30 pm that afternoon. Although she was walking into the unknown, the joy of being shortlisted meant that she was almost there. He liked her; she knew it — there was hope.

On the bus ride to the Soto residence Viola slipped into a reverie, calming her inner waters to be present in the moment when she met the child. Everything rested on her shoulders now. Sebastian could continue his incognito exploits, but she had to deliver what Tempest ordered. She craved a stick of peanut brittle but let the moment pass to avoid clouding her judgement. She summoned her inner strength with the mantra, *you got this.*

Dressed in black ballet flats, black formal pants, and a pale blue, willowy blouse with her hair tamed in a ponytail, she exuded a youthful freshness on this warm Athenian afternoon. She pressed the buzzer aware of the close circuit camera whizzing above her head to let her know she was watched when she heard Soto's voice.

'Ah Ms Bardo, I will be with you in a second.'

He opened the door as she adjusted her ponytail. His dress was more casual this afternoon, jeans, and a white sweatshirt with a tuft of gray hair visible above his crew neck collar. He welcomed her with an extended arm which he placed on her elbow to guide her through the doorway.

'Come in, it's much cooler in here. What a hot afternoon!'

'Thank you, Mr Soto, it sure is a hot one.'

'Please take a seat, I'll be back.' He nodded and stepped backwards out the door.

Viola was under no illusions — she knew there were eyes watching her every move from somewhere in the house.

A clickety-clack of hard heels approached the office where Soto had left her.

Then a mellow voice said from behind her, 'Hello, Ms Bardo.'

Viola stood up to attention, turned around and extended her hand, 'Good afternoon.'

'I'm Bernice, I've been the child's carer for Matthew — a temporary role.'

She also used the word *child* — it was clear the child was a boy but neither Matthew nor Bernice referred to him by name. Bernice had an American accent which she tried to conceal without success. She did not mention her familial connection to Soto, but her face was an older female version of his — genes were hard to conceal. Both had a cultured air of politeness, making it difficult to believe they were capable of kidnapping a child. White collar crime existed in various shapes and forms, appearance and reality were contenders in the assignments Viola worked on for Tempest. This would be a tip-toe around the reasons why they took the child. There she was doing it now, thinking of the boy as *the child*. Keeping up appearances was part of her expectation, while she would prefer a less restrained environment, she had to maintain an air of formality. She sat erect in her chair, pulled in her chin, and inclined her head, intent on catching every word Bernice uttered, while hoping she did not appear overly inquisitive.

'Matthew will be present in your meeting with *the child*, I'll keep in the background,' then she added should *the boy* become anxious with Viola's presence, only then would she intervene to settle him. She stepped backwards out the door just as Matthew did.

Tiny, quick footsteps hurried down the corridor, Viola could hear heavy footsteps for every five little steps. She straightened her shoulders, rolled her neck around to ease the tightness and walked to the door.

A beautiful round-faced child with striking eyes against a rush of shiny golden hair floated into the room and stopped dead in his tracks when he saw her. His blue eyes gleamed in an unsure smile. Matthew let go of the child's hand.

'Say hello to Ms Bardo,' Matthew urged, and then repeated the line in German with not a hint of his American accent.

The boy cocked his head to the left, looked up at Viola and said, 'Hullo Ms Bardo.'

'Ms Bardo, this is Junge,' Viola walked towards him and touched his arm. He extended his little hand to shake hers. At last she had a face and a name and what an adorable lad Junge was — polite and pleasant just the way she hoped he would be.

'Show Ms Bardo what you've been painting.' Junge rushed out the room to get his paint book.

'The first part of this meeting appears to be moving along well,' Matthew Soto said in a full-toothed grin.

She was keen to ask why his name was Junge and stopped when she heard little feet running back to the office.

Viola sat on the floor paging through his artwork with Matthew looking on. Bernice stood at the back of the room with a watchful eye. Appearance was no longer an issue in the company of an animated child who spoke with pride of his mini masterpieces. Matthew translated some of Junge's

German phrases and told her his English was getting better every day. A warm maternal glow tugged at her — she knew she could not fall in love with this child and yet how could anyone not feel a swirl of compassion in knowing his mother had died not so long ago.

The boy showed no signs of trauma and appeared calm while she was in the house. She felt guilty for her deception, but the child had to be returned unharmed to his father. After a pleasant hour lost in a child's make-believe world, it was time for Viola to depart. Junge waved saying something in German which Matthew explained meant, come back soon.

The time with Junge made her nostalgic. As an only child she knew loneliness. She had many imaginary friends. Her father encouraged her to forge close friendships, but her mother forbade it. It was better to remain reclusive, playing with imagined mates. Endless tea parties for one was her childhood fun and her father and his friends went along with her make-believe world. Seeing Junge brought those memories flooding back, rekindling her compassionate muse.

Straddling two countries
Both home to you
Language is not a barrier
In your blue-eyed innocence
Amid an international fracas
Eternally smile little one
Keep your spirit white as the dove
Brimming with love
Joy will be yours soon
Never fear — look to the moon
For strife
Is not a child's life

SHE SAUNTERED along Plaka with these lines filling her head in a blur of confusion on why someone who was obviously intelligent and caring like Matthew Soto would do what he did by unlawfully removing Junge from his father — the word kidnapper did not match the character. The lad had a fondness for Soto that Viola was keen to understand. She knew deception when called to protect the ones we love for she withheld information from her mother on her father's activities to avoid him being persecuted for his lifestyle. Would the crime have been unresolved, or how long would Matthew's plan have lasted had Tempest not intervened?

SOON SHE WAS outside Sebastian's apartment block, he met her in the foyer. He was fresh and rested compared to the mental and emotional exhaustion she felt.

'We have to speak to Tempest now that I have proof that the child is in Soto's care.'

'Yes, that's why I cooked us a homemade dinner as a time saver to action these steps to prepare for what comes next. Grilled Texan style chicken and quinoa, blistered tomatoes and avocado salad are on offer.'

'You've been a busy boy, I see. That sounds delicious, thank you.'

IN UNDER AN HOUR, dinner was down with a glass of sparkling water and, Tempest was on the line.

'Greetings team!'

'Good evening Tempest,' they both greeted with the enthusiasm of Charlie's angels.

'How was your afternoon in Soto's den?'

'Interesting, he's polite and taking good care of the child, I'll give him that from what I've observed.'

'I know you will pull it off if he takes you on as governess.'

Viola issued heaps of praise upon her students and being on the receiving end of praise from Tempest was a good feeling.

SEBASTIAN CALLED a cab for her return to Aurora. It was 8:30 pm. She needed a bath and had some lesson preparation to complete before bed.

Soto's message came through while she bathed — the job was hers and he expected her to start on Monday morning.

13

The Prime Minister's son was waiting outside her classroom that morning, smiling like there was no catastrophe surrounding him. In class he continued in his usual unruffled manner perhaps unaware that the headmaster called an emergency meeting in his honor. There was no further meeting to explain that he would be back in class. Students were blissfully oblivious to the situation around the Sanchez boy. Staff remained tight-lipped. Viola was bursting to know what had happened to Brendan Sanchez.

And so, the school day passed like any other with not a hair raised and not a word said.

* * *

Earlier that day...

She dreaded informing Miles Alexakis that the time had come to have her agreed few days off school. He was busy with paperwork piled high on his desk when she knocked on his door. His personal assistant was on a day's leave, so she had easy access to him.

'Good afternoon Ms Bardo, this is a surprise, is everything OK?'

'Yes, well, now that Brandon Sanchez is back at school and unharmed.'

Miles gave her a furtive look. He nodded and looked down at his mountain of paperwork. With a chilly tenseness he asked, 'Is there anything I can help you with today?'

'I wanted to let you know in person that I am taking three days off next week as agreed.'

'Thank you, yes I remember on your first day here that you mentioned you might need some days off. That's in order, I will let my PA know to get you cover for those days.' His sudden icy to warm attitude baffled her. She missed Rob Dwyer. He was constant most of the time at Blackwater Ridge Performing Arts Academy. Staff who understood him avoided interactions when he barricaded himself in his office. With Viola his door was always open. He moved on from staff issues, never bearing a grudge. Here leadership turned staff into nocturnal creatures, hidden by day, in unspoken secrecy. It was never an area of school life that appealed to her — she enjoyed the freedom to come and go as she wanted or as Tempest expected.

'Thank you, Mr Alexakis, I will be at a friend's place so I'm reachable should anything require my attention during those days.'

'Thank you for the consideration, I will inform my PA. It's a pity you will miss our German visitor's presentation at the school assembly. Have a pleasant few days away.'

He continued with his work shutting out any further conversation.

Interesting man, with his political connections, and aloof personality! His political ally was arriving next week, and she would miss his visit. It convinced her that his association with the German Ambassador had some intertwining vines. Miles was *Heathcliff-ean* — dark, but she hoped not terrible. She felt a haiku coming on to describe his brevity.

A cold man of stone
On an alabaster throne
Alone in control

THAT SUMMED up her experience with him. The formality at Aurora was stifling for an Aussie girl who thought of everyone as a mate on a first name basis — if she met the president of any country she would call them by their first name with ease. 'Hello Barack,' was one such desire. Rob was Rob although she chose to maintain formality in addressing him at work — that's the way she knew, that's how her father raised her. Aurora was a fortress and Miles its only gatekeeper. Her gratitude was for the friendship she shared with Maria and Vince. His quirky ways made her welcome in an institution that erected walls between people.

TO ANTICIPATE something new or something different, makes time pass like an unwatched clock. The bell at the end of the school day jolted her out of her reverie — nothing distinct, just a hazy cloud of nothingness floated through her for most of the day. She walked back to the teachers' quarters and found a note pinned to her front door. Vince wanted her to join him for a home-cooked dinner at six-thirty that evening. He promised a gastronomical delight that she should not miss. The distraction of his company was what she needed, but she had to let him know she would be away next week. She would spin a yarn on what she was doing with her time off because he would ask. Vince would back off if she was not forthcoming on the specifics of her absence.

Maria came over with scones from the fresh batch she had baked for the boarding house afternoon tea. Viola's itch to know more was uncontrollable. The prime person with an easy tongue, not quite an Aurora brainwashed inmate, was at her mercy.

'The Sanchez boy is back in class today like nothing happened.'

'Yes, everybody is mum about it, I suppose I better keep my mouth shut too.'

'I thought you might have some news on that, I didn't realize that you were also in the dark.'

'Lord knows I've been here enough years to know when to be quiet. I'll be honest, I'm as curious as the next person, but retirement beckons and I don't want any fuss because I let a word slip, you know.'

'I understand, do what you have to do.'

'I noticed the boy's chauffeur going into Mr Alexakis' office yesterday morning though. He was there for almost an hour. Some secret meeting perhaps! Ooh, I would have loved to be a fly on that wall. Perhaps it is better that I don't know what they met to discuss.'

'Interesting.'

'Mr Alexakis asked me to bring in coffee for his guest so while I was not a fly on the wall, I was the pink elephant in some ways!' She chuckled and Viola enjoyed this carefree side of Maria. 'He never has guests in his private office. It has always been the conference room. Odd really odd!'

Viola knew Maria's claim of ignorance would be short-lived. She was the eyes and ears of the school. The faucet was open and there was no stopping her gush. She meant no harm at all, just needed company, somebody who did not talk over her like the teenagers she served every day. Viola listened with enjoyment.

For a second she wondered whether Sebastian observed that the boy had returned to school, did he track how he got home and then to school?

'I am pleased that the student is back and bears no physical hurt.'

'Aren't you lovely, Ms Bardo! We need more of you around here.' She shook her head and a sad wistful look dimmed the light in her eyes. She continued, 'Mr Alexakis called late yesterday to say he has a foreign diplomat visiting the school, so some menu arrangements need attention.'

Viola buttered a scone while it was still hot, trying not to be overtly curious about what Maria knew about the foreign visitor to the school.

'These are delicious, Maria, I love them.'

'I could bring you more later, I have to hurry now before the boarders head off for their afternoon activities.'

'This will do me, please bring no more — I might need a new wardrobe if I eat anymore!'

'See you later, or rather chat to you later, if you are on campus tonight.' Her lingering smile let Viola know that Maria was onto her movements, perhaps suspecting she had a love interest somewhere in Athens.

She downloaded a few fairy tales to entertain Junge and popped her earphones in to listen to some English-German translations. Exhaustion claimed her and soon she fell into a deep sleep.

Her early childhood in Lourenço Marques with her French African mother, and African Portuguese father was a colorful time in her life, before the nastiness preceding their divorce. Her head had the same loose curl as her mother but her pale skin tone was her father's. Her mother's caramel skin under-tones gave her an exotic European look. Her father fondly called her mother his dark sultry one. Viola wished her family had remained together but as she grew and matured, she real-ized how destructive their personalities were to each other. Both artists needing mindful energy to sustain their creativity. She accepted that it was as it had to be.

She walked through the markets with her father every Saturday morning, to purchase a tin of his favorite *peri-peri* cashew nuts. Her mother called him frivolous for dragging Viola around the busy markets.

On one such market trip while she waited for her father to collect his *peri-peri* roasted nuts, she observed the young man in the next stall. His impish grin and pixie ears enticed her to stare at him. He called her over and she let go of her father's hand and reached out to accept the blood red apple he offered her. He rolled his large bright eyes like a ventriloquist's doll, shaking his spring-loaded head. She saw thumbs on both his hands, and webbed fingers, flat and thin-skinned. Yet he held the apple with a dexterous vice grip to prevent it rolling away, he released the grip on the apple when he knew she was holding it. It troubled her all day until she asked her father why his hands were that way. Her father explained that it might have been a birth defect and perhaps his family could not afford to rectify it with surgery. She recalled her sadness, 'Please, papa help him, make him have fingers like me, please.' Her sobbing found no end and her father's heart melted. He first explained that people sometimes, did not want interfer-ence from outsiders in their private lives, as the young man seemed to want. Nothing more was said about the young man until they moved to Australia. Her father contacted the young stall owner and they got to know Elio when he accepted the offer of surgery to rectify the deformity and physiotherapy to learn to use his hands with five separated fingers. Elio visited them twice in Australia until one day they received shocking news that soldiers had gunned him down during an uprising at the market. The Frelimo terrorists lived in her memory of seeing them lined up along the roadside close to the border checkpoint — armed and silent. Elio was an undercover freedom fighter, and someone sold him out to the rebels. She recalled the mangy dog on the dilapidated iron bridge baring its teeth in hunger and she was desperate to offer it food. When she saw struggle and suffering, something within called out to her to ease the pain others felt, in whatever way she could.

During this time travel dream, she heard her doorbell ring in the distance, then a gentle thumping on her door. She opened her eyes. It was pitch black around her; she had slept for at least three hours without stirring.

Vince called out to her.

'Viola! Have you forgotten about dinner? It won't stay warm for much longer. Are you coming over now?'

He took advantage of his loud voice with no other teachers in their little neighborhood.

'Give me ten minutes, sorry Vince, I'll freshen up and be over,' she called back from behind a locked front door. She had no reason to lock her door here, but her parents' insistence on keeping their Mozambiqan doors shut was a habit.

'Dinner awaits, madam, so don't bother freshening up, my lights are dim, and my eyes will be closed,' he exclaimed in a French accent.

A splash of water on her face, a dab of lip gloss and her hair twisted in a tight knot was all she needed. She was a natural beauty as her mother's daughter. She rushed back into her bedroom, sprayed herself in a cloud of deodorant before dashing out.

'Thank you for dinner, I must apologize for my tardiness. I've been working too hard this week and what I planned as a quick nap became the big sleep.' She squeezed his arm, and he pretended to sulk with a childish pout, shook his head and clicked his scolding tongue. Vince brought her back to the real world. His fun-loving energy was a blessing.

'You have been a ghost this week, the last I caught sight of you was at that emergency staff meeting. Now the boy's back and silence has sealed all lips — that's Aurora for you! Live and learn every day. Eat up now, there's enough to feed an army.' He waltzed around the table, poured himself a glass of red which she refused opting for water instead.

She told him she had taken a few days off and would not be on the campus.

'Always on the go is our Australian mystery lady, on some secret mission then?'

'Nothing secret,' she blushed on that lie, just some personal matters that need attention.'

'I'll let you have your space but do hurry back, I need your sanity around here.'

He had no idea how therapeutic he was for her.

LATER THAT NIGHT she packed a bag and sneaked out to Sebastian's place, relieved that George was on gate duty. He knew she was on a few days leave.

Vince's mystery lady comment left her naked and stung.

14

F ive days...

VIOLA ARRIVED at Matthew Soto's place at 7:30 am. She had taken up residence for the next three days at Sebastian's apartment. For her it was awkward, for him, it meant they could have in-house meetings without wandering the streets of Athens.

Her contract with Soto stipulated her working day from eight in the morning to four-thirty in the afternoon. This gave her the flexibility to convene with Sebastian and Tempest with no delays in sharing information.

'GOOD MORNING, MS BARDO,' Soto greeted her in a cheery voice, but the formality of his address kept her at arm's length. 'Punctual as always, thank you! I'm leaving in fifteen minutes, but I slip in and out during the day, so I hope that won't affect your schedule with Junge. He's in the kitchen with Bernice and eager to spend the day with you. She will be close throughout the day. Please avail yourself to whatever you would like to eat or drink but as per the contract, no smoking and alcohol on duty.'

Aye, aye captain, but the words that left her lips were, 'Thank you, Mr Soto, that's most kind of you. My only vice is a peanut brittle addiction,' she laughed and then regretted saying it for how foolish it sounded.

'Please don't offer any of it to Junge, too much sugar sets him off for a sleepless night, his energy is difficult to contain as it is.'

'That won't happen.' Her cheeks burned and his piercing look confirmed that her peanut brittle vice was unnecessary information!

'One more thing, for today, do not take the boy outdoors.'

First his energy is difficult to contain and now do not take the boy outdoors. How was this having a childhood at all? She gave him a searching look — what could he be hiding from her — she was sure as hell going to find out. Then realization struck, the German Ambassador, Junge's father, was in town so Soto was playing it safe. She turned on her listening device for Sebastian to note any irregularities that might occur on her first day as an au pair. Today he was snooping around the school vicinity to observe the happenings around the Ambassador's visit.

JUNGE SAT at the kitchen counter with his legs swaying back and forth gaining momentum when he saw her. He jumped off his seat, landed on his knees, winced, got up and made a dash for Viola, calling out. 'Ms Bardo!' He wanted a hug, like one would expect from a mother. Although startled by his overt display of affection, she responded with a bear-hug.

'Hey Junge, how are you this morning, what are you eating? You can call me Viola now.'

'Viola-Viola! Oats.'

'Yum! I love oats.' She regretted saying that because he insisted she tasted some from his bowl. Soto would hate this, so she refused saying she had already had too much breakfast.

He reached for a high five and blurted out, 'Big Ted show me.'

'Did Big Ted teach you how to high five?'

'Ja.'

Bernice was tidying up the kitchen when Viola walked in, she greeted her from the kitchen sink. She turned around expecting to be asked a few questions on Big Ted.

'Big Ted is a friend's son. He comes over sometimes to play with Junge. He loves Playschool and sees himself as Little Ted.' She turned away before Viola could ask any questions.

'That's good that he has a friend come over.'

With her back still turned Bernice mumbled, 'He won't come around now that you're here.'

Another odd reaction, to stop the child's friend from coming over because the child has a governess... It was not so much that Aurora, as an institution, was odd — it was the people she encountered who had hidden agendas.

At 9 am Viola had her first English lesson with Junge. Bernice went off to shower and dress. Basic naming of concrete objects in the room helped her gain a sense of where to begin with extending her student's language skills. Association was key to unlocking his understanding. Junge pulled her arm to lead her to his room to show her he could name most things there. He said, 'bed' and 'sleep' together and closed his eyes in the most angelic way that made her want to hug him. His bedroom was down a long passage, the entrance hidden from a cursory look that way. The room was decorated with every toy imaginable — a large aeroplane was suspended above his bed. A large toy box with everything a little boy would desire spilt out onto the green carpet. Puzzles, Lego, a miniature sports car collection, a racing track in a box, a train track running along the walls of the room. The little bookshelf caught her eye, it was stacked with picture books. This gained Matthew Soto kudos in her book. The thing that troubled her was, that there was no natural light in the room — there were no windows!

Junge picked up an iPad and scrolled through the photographs with his little fingers moving in quick deliberate motion from left to right. Then he shouted out with excitement, 'Big Ted! Big Ted!'

THE FACE of the boy with his arms around Junge, was Brendan Sanchez!

'Is this your friend, Big Ted?'

'Ja, Big Ted gone.' His smile vanished. He loved his friend, there was no doubt about that. Viola needed to know when Big Ted came over to the house. At this point it was difficult to get Junge to give her this information.

Bernice coughed in the doorway announcing her presence — how long was she standing there, how much did she hear? Viola was skilled at composing herself in an instant.

Bernice ignored Viola and spoke to Junge, 'Come it's time to play now, come along.'

'Viola-Viola come play!'

AT MIDDAY JUNGE watched Playschool and sang along to all the ditties and repeated the nursery rhymes with mimicked expertize. Viola noted an announcement at the bottom of the television screen. It read — *Ambassador Frankel arrived in Athens today.*

Viola did not hear Matthew Soto arrive until he was in the room standing behind her.

'Hello Ms Bardo, how are things?'

'It's going very well, thank you. We're having a lot of fun.'

Junge rushed over to Soto the minute he heard his voice. Soto picked him up and enfolded him in his arms.

'You're having a good day, with Ms Bardo, ja.'

Junge nodded, 'Viola-Viola!'

'Are you happy with him calling you by your first name, Ms Bardo?'

She almost blurted out, at last somebody is, but was careful, 'Absolutely, no issues with that.'

Matthew spent fifteen minutes with Junge and left.

The telephone rang in the kitchen and Viola assumed it was Soto, perhaps he had forgotten something.

Bernice picked up the telephone and put it down after the second 'hello.'

'Pranksters!'

'Does that happen often?'

'Twice yesterday, around this time and later in the afternoon. It's never happened before yesterday.'

'Ask Mr Soto to monitor it, put a trace on it if it's persistent.'

'Must be school kids being naughty, that's all.'

It confused Viola that she would think it was a school kid when school was still in for the day.

Viola's mobile screen lit up. It was a message from Vince with a cross-eyed selfie. *Lucky fish, you missed the most boring pomp and ceremony in assembly today!* His emoticons made her want to laugh out loud, but she had to be cautious under the watchful eye of Bernice whose surname was unknown. The German Ambassador, Frankel, now she had a name, seemed to have visited Aurora directly on his way from the airport.

She left that afternoon after a ceremonious hug from Junge. On her way out, she noted a black sedan parked across from the house. When she turned to note the occupants and registration number of the vehicle — the windows buzzed up to shut out her curious eyes. Five minutes on her walk to see Sebastian, the vehicle cruised past her again.

SEBASTIAN MET her at the fountain in Syntagma Square, it was a bright afternoon and she needed to be outdoors after being locked in all day.

'How was your first day as a governess? I kept looking out to see if you had a brolly and took to flying, *Ms Poppins!*'

Viola laughed much to Sebastian's surprise, she detested being called a nanny and his allusion to Mary Poppins, his childish poke at her, did not offend. He was the little brother she never had, making fun at her expense. She saw this relationship between her father and his sister, Lorenza.

'I had a great day, thank you, but I think I was being followed when I left the house.'

This grabbed Sebastian's attention, '*Think* you were, or *were* you followed, please be direct.'

The little brother disappeared, and the curious detective surfaced.

She explained that the black sedan might have been on the street all day and perhaps was not following her after all.

'I think the house is being watched, a set-up by the foreign Ambassador. It is his child that's missing and as much as he might have asked Tempest to investigate for him, he would have people snooping around. Power chooses how and when to control. On another note, you will be happy to know I slipped into Aurora's assembly today for the Ambassador's presentation.'

'How did you manage that?' Viola looked at him in disbelief.

'Long story. I did a bit of investigation prior to his arrival. It was a backdoor entry. I called the catering company, the school had booked and asked for job vacancies. I landed a waiter position right inside Aurora today! How's that for you?'

'Wait, take a step back, please, you have my head spinning. How did you get all this information?'

His impish grin had Viola in a panic, he failed at his door-to-door salesman attempt and now he got into Aurora, past the security. She had to sign in and out each time she left and arrived, and she was staff!

'I called the catering department at the school, your friend Maria chirped that they had already booked a caterer for the day and when I asked which company she sang like a nightingale. I didn't want you to ask questions to compromise your position as staff.'

'It's already compromised, I daresay! But please protect Maria at all costs, she wants to retire soon and does not need negative publicity before this. She's a lovely soul.'

'And safe she shall remain. Who would want to stay on in that place is my question? Its stiff and Maria seemed like the only ultra-cool person there.'

'You have done well, Sebastian sir!' She bowed and doffed her imaginary cap.

He wanted to know about her day; she told him that Bernice was on watchdog duty and she was prohibited outdoor activities with the Junge. Sebastian asked who Big Ted was and Viola needed to have her moment of mystery, a small victory over his ingenious entry into Aurora.

'Well, would you like to guess who he is?'

'No please tell me, too much suspense ruins my appetite!'

'It's Brendan Sanchez.'

'Your student? The Prime Minister's son?'

'Yes.'

'Now we know for sure where he was when reported missing. The pieces are coming together very well, Ms Bardo!'

'Tell me what the day was like behind the majestic gates of Aurora.'

'Miles appeared chummy with the Ambassador, leaning over, speaking into his ear, laughing together. I don't know how the man can laugh when his little boy is missing and in the middle of an international investigation.'

'Politicians, what more can I say? Did you hear the Ambassador's speech?'

'He's a friend of the school, if you know that I mean, he sang Aurora's praises to sickening heights. The interesting thing is he added that Aurora is his wife's alma mater. It was as if she was not dead, but if she was Soto's sister, she is American, so why would she attend a school in Athens?'

Viola agreed that this interesting piece of information was more confounding than clear and warranted further investigation. Sebastian told her Tempest wanted to talk to them.

AFTER DINNER TEMPEST'S voice breezed in. Viola and Sebastian had their headphones in place.

'Good evening! You have done well to get this far, team.'

'My job is not over until Junge is with his father.' Viola's furrowed brow added ten years to her.

'If that is the right thing to do, we must dig into the Ambassador's world a little more, I am onto it and will give you the update soon. My contact should return this to me in two hours.'

This threw Viola for a second. The task was to return the boy unharmed to his family in Germany. Now the goal post took on another dimension.

Tempest announced at midnight that the Ambassador had remarried an Athenian woman, two months after his wife's, Junge's mother's death. She was half his age and did not accompany him on any official business matters and no information was available on what she looked like or who she was.

15

Four Days

Viola arrived early for day two as Junge's governess — a role she was quite enjoying.

Nobody was home.

Windows were shut, blinds drawn, and leaves gathered in forlorn bundles along the driveway.

The house appeared like it stood that way, vacant for many years.

Yesterday's joy, now a shadow.

Viola was rooted to the spot in disbelief, considering whether her mind was tricking her with her worst fear — so close, FOUR DAYS — FOUR DAYS thrummed in her head. She stepped away from the latched front gate and peered down the driveway. A gust of wind teased her curly brown locks, pushing it across her eyes. She shoved her hair out of the way and walked halfway up the driveway when she noticed a book flapping in a wild frenzy. It was Junge's art book, his treasured art book — forgotten after an obvious hurried departure. Then she felt a tingling sensation at the back of her neck. She spun around expecting to see someone, the menacing black sedan cruised past. The impenetrable blackness behind the tinted windows hid the secret occupants from view.

SOMETHING HAD HAPPENED OVERNIGHT, and she had no answers.
Matthew, Bernice and Junge gone!

SHE RUSHED out the driveway onto the street only to catch the sedan's tail end as it turned out of sight. Who is this and why was the car cruising past the house for the second day in a row? Were they looking for her? Why? She called Sebastian and hurried to meet him at their usual spot at the fountain. The sight and sound of flowing water was vital to soothing her fraught nerves. A crowd of tourists gathered on the opposite side of the fountain with a loud boisterous tour guide invading her thinking space. The group became a mob of colorful clothes in her mental search for answers. Sebastian suggested going to his apartment to debrief in peace.

'HOW CAN THAT BE, it looks like nobody's lived there for years, it's an abandoned ghostly house? This has messed my head, badly!'

Sebastian listened, staring not seeing, thinking, pondering, wondering. A light breeze entered through the open balcony door, tips of his hair, dead center on his head, stood like antennae searching for a signal. He shook his head in his mental conversation.

'Speak to me, I need your thoughts on this, please. Today was the day I should have taken Junge to his father.'

'Sorry, Viola, this is a shock. All I can say is that this has something to do with the Ambassador's visit here. Think carefully, was there anything out of the ordinary when you were there yesterday.'

'To be honest, everything was out of the ordinary, I was not allowed to take the boy outside, had to hold him captive indoors, he had a bedroom with no outfacing windows, well no windows at all! Bernice watched my every move. Then there was the silent caller who apparently according to Bernice was calling twice a day for the last two days.'

'Either the Ambassador has something to do with this, or Matthew Soto has them in hiding.'

'I hope the latter is correct, then at least Junge will be safe.'

'Do you really think so? Has Soto earned this respect, this belief you have in him?'

'Only from his protective, warm and loving interactions with the child.'

'I have news for you, not as a doomsayer but, historically we have known the most heinous serial killers to have led relatively normal family lives.'

'True. My gut tells me there's more underpinning Soto's reason for taking the child out of Germany with no prior parental consent. He is not stupid. He knows how the law operates and that this is at great peril to himself.'

'I did some snooping last night after you went to bed. Actually, a friend is doing the snooping for me as we speak. He is a German national, a trusted contact. I have him looking into new marriage records filed in the last two years in Germany.'

'Why are you involving an outsider? While this might be what we need, we should inform Tempest about outside interference in the case. I hope we have some leads soon. We are nearing the twelfth day and now this crops up!'

'I will speak to Tempest on this. My contact does not know why I want the information, if he asks, I will say it's part of my sabbatical research.'

Viola did not want to argue with him, if he was going to inform Tempest that is all she needed to know.

Each retreated to a private space in the small apartment that afternoon. Sebastian scrolled through online newspapers picking up whatever he could on the Prime Minister, but not much was available on the Ambassador.

It was a warm afternoon. He poured them both a gin and tonic which Viola declined.

'You need to lighten up, Ms Bardo, you are not at Aurora now. I'll get you an apple juice. I have more information to share.'

Sebastian returned with a jug of chilled apple juice and pushed his gin and tonic aside.

'You're right, we need a clear head, not a relaxed one with this new development. I called a cleaning company that services Parliament House, they need a new staff member, so I secured an interview at 4:30 pm today.

'What? That's in an hour! How did you do that with the security and secrecy around the services they use?'

'The advertisement for the position did not say it was for Parliament House, but the wording of the notice and location seemed to suggest it was, to me anyway, and I was right!'

'You have a knack of worming your way into situations. It sounds good, you better hurry along and thankfully you rethought that gin!' She pulled her feet up onto the couch and laughed.

Sebastian was happy that her gloom had lifted.

'I have to brief Tempest on the situation.'

'Yeah, and I have to return to Aurora tomorrow.

Viola's anxiety surfaced in her concern for Junge's whereabouts — had she missed some crucial clue while she was at Soto's house? The child took most of her attention. She considered whether Junge's friend, Big Ted, had any answers on the mysterious disappearance of the child and two adults. Being away from Aurora was not assisting the advancement of the case. She had to observe Brendan's, alias Big Ted's, behavior during this time.

IN AN UNKNOWN LOCATION on the other side of the world, Tempest wafted around in her ethereal way. Her canary yellow kaftan billowed up behind her. She looked out at the endless stretch of sea — a sight that greeted her all day, every day. It was a brilliant clear day made to be outdoors, but she had to provide answers, or at the very least offer a few clues for Sebastian and Viola to find Junge and get him out of Athens. The original brief issued had nose-dived. At fifty-eight Tempest could easily pass for a woman ten years younger. Her unlined, olive skin and slim silhouette whittled a few years. Her hair, now long flowing dreadlocks, cascaded down her back. She had soft light brown hair, full lips, big hazel eyes, and a rather pert nose. Her solitary life in this massive beach house gave her the anonymity that was necessary but never desired. After being the fresh face of journalism as a woman of color, here she was, isolated from face-to-face human contact. She was a fading memory to the rest of the world but her fighting spirit against injustice was as alive as it was in her youth. Viola and Sebastian were her voice and action agents on matters that disturbed her. She was brusque when a job had to be done. Emotions never clouded her judgement. Viola and Sebastian brought a freshness to her life passion and blunted her loneliness.

In between her research, investigations and issuing instructions to her agents she lost herself in painting. Her easel stood commandingly erect on the balcony, sea-facing for there is where she drew inspiration. Outside those hours she was writing her memoir which would be her posthumous publication — she could not publish before that — there was too much at risk. She toyed with titles, *The Other Life*, or *What might have been*, but decided to defer that to when she had completed her memoir.

Living in isolation was difficult but her parrot, Caramba, was a keen white watcher of the skies and her two Rottweilers, Khaya and Woza filled her lonely hours. As their names suggested, one was watchful as Khaya, for her safe return home, and Woza, contrary to her name, was forever restful, never getting enough sleep. While Khaya trotted beside her on her early morning walk and Caramba kept a steadfast eye on what was up ahead, Woza slept on the shore close to the house burying her nose in the warm sand, waiting for the trio's return. Caramba's scolding squawk was a sign for Woza to get moving. Tempest had a scarf at the ever ready during her beach walks. When Caramba swooped onto her shoulder, she knew it was time to pull the scarf over her head to conceal her identity from approaching human presence on this isolated strip of beach. This was her daylight daily ritual. Such was her menagerie, a world that she held private away from public gaze.

A perpetual order of the same groceries paid for in advance arrived at her gate every Friday. With no personal human interactions, she trusted that her food would be there like clockwork each week. She grew her own vegetables and herbs to supplement her vegetarian diet. Living at the front door of the ocean did not tempt a pescatarian palate. Khaya and Woza were treated to stewed lamb and generous bones with fresh herbs added from her lush garden. One sound-proofed room in this vast abode housed her high-tech communications equipment to keep her pulse on the world while it had lost hers. Her communications system allowed her to breeze in and out of connection with Viola and Sebastian.

Late nights saw her back on the balcony listening to the swish of waves as it broke on the shore while she puffed on an apple and cinnamon tobacco pipe. She developed this habit, a craving now, to soothe her nerves and fragile emotions and, continued her late-night puffs which sometimes had her in a fit of coughing — chastisements in her former years were no longer there to caution her about health matters. Now she accepted that you only live once and a few pleasures, if it did not harm anyone, was good enough.

TEMPEST KICKED OFF HER SANDALS, pulled both feet up onto her desk chair ready for a virtual meeting with Viola and Sebastian. An hour before the briefing Sebastian returned to his apartment with a smile so big and bright, ready to electrify Athens. The interview was a success, the job was his, and he was asked to start the next day — nights only. He impressed the interview panel, to be appointed assistant head cleaner at Parliament House.

'You must have mesmerized them to land that position, well done!' Viola reached over to high-five her colleague for his ingeniousness. Then she added in playful jest, 'Please apply those cleaning skills to your own apartment.' She cast a condemning glance around the room like a mother inspecting her child's mess.

'Who said official cleaners had to have clean homes? Dare I say that teachers are as wise as their subjects... oops, cancel that, I did not say that, I am blabbering on in excitement!' He held his hands up for Viola's forgiveness.

On that note, Tempest floated into their communication cyberspace.

'Good evening team, glad to see that securing such a job brings you lots of thrills. A jovial mood prevails.'

'Good evening, Tempest,' they chirped as second nature to a kindergarten class.

'At this point I don't have conclusive information on the boy's whereabouts, but I am losing my patience with his father!'

This was a first, hearing annoyance articulated against her client. They both waited in quiet patience for her next point.

'How can a father show such a lack of concern when his child is missing? In this world today when a child goes missing the radar should be on high alert — too much impacts the lives of missing children, who end up dead, or scarred for life. What choice is that? Bah! Call himself a father?'

Sebastian spoke first, 'Perhaps he is enjoying being a celebrity, living the high life of indulgence here in Athens.'

'His priorities must be from his own screwed past. How do you serve a nation if you can't serve your own family, right? His selfish indulgence makes him suspicious in my book!' Viola could not withhold this outburst.

'Agreed! Wonderful, Viola!' This was another first — Tempest rarely supported opinions with such zeal or with overt personal compliments. Viola needed to hear those words, for it was only her father who praised his Artista this way.

Tempest's agents secretly enjoyed her human side.

'We can accomplish much in four days. I leave you to it. I will be in touch.'

Off she went, into the vortex, for a while.

Sebastian gave Viola a clownish lopsided grin. He checked that Tempest was offline before he said, 'Tempest was, shall I say, wild or wild tempered tonight!'

'Her relaxed manner was a surprise but lovely to hear. She must know something that she cannot divulge just yet, perhaps the reason for letting down her guard.'

'Women's intuition, I suppose, but I don't have experience on that,' he grinned, 'other than from what I read.'

'Congrats again on the cleaning job, and a senior position! So do you just turn up tomorrow?'

'I have to pick up the overall and identification tag tomorrow morning.'

'Finally, I will see you in a suit!'

'No possibility of that happening! I'm not leaving this building dressed in that outfit!'

'Make sure you let Tempest know about the investigating friend you added into the quotient.'

'I will when the time is right.'

LONG AFTER MIDNIGHT Sebastian received news from his German contact on recent marriages in Germany. The list was long but the one he was waiting for, was the Ambassador's marriage to an Athenian woman.

Her maiden name was Alexakis! Arielle Madonna Alexakis!

The Aurora connection had sprung another leaf!

16

D ay three

BACK AT AURORA everything ran like clockwork — Vince and Maria were the only ones happy to see Viola back in the teachers' residence.

Viola was edgy about reporting her return to Miles. It was unnecessary but it was her polite way. He was Junge's step-uncle, and that added layers of complications rather than Miles' awareness of her involvement in the kidnapping investigation.

Another hiccup was Brendan Sanchez — how would he react to his little mate's disappearance? Would he be at school today? She was eager to get to her first class; she missed her students, and needed the pulse from that passion, Brendan had crept into her heart as a child being used in the political situation around Junge — a complicated life for a fourteen-year-old.

Year Nine lined up outside Viola's classroom, she expected Brendan would straggle in at the end of the line.

He was not at school.

Her professionalism would hold her back from asking why he was away. The tight-lipped community would remain mute. Maria might say something in her wonderful innocence, she hoped.

Her class was still that morning, she was sitting with a little group at the piano at the back of the room, when she heard a faint knock. Jace Dimakos, awkward, and hesitant, peered into the room, searching for her, swaying from foot to the other. She walked towards him while he adjusted his glasses. He reminded her of a teenage boy on his first day in high school.

As was Aurora's way in the junior years, the class sang out when they saw the assistant head at the door, 'Good morning, Mr Dimakos!' Jace raised his hand without returning the greeting. He took a few steps towards Viola across the threshold of the entrance. His raised eyebrows lowered his glasses onto his slender nose.

Viola felt the familiar gyration in her belly and quickened her pace sensing that something was amiss. She turned to her students in mid-step and instructed, 'Work on without a sound, class, I'll be coming around to your groups soon,' her jovial tone hid her anxiety. Had the school authorities discovered her undercover role? Was she getting her marching orders? Did Miles want to see her in his office? The contortion in her stomach tightened in a knot.

'Oh, hello, Ms Bardo... good to see you back. Did you have a relaxing few days?'

'Yes I did thank you...,' she lied, halting herself from calling him by his first name, 'thanks for asking, Mr Dimakos.' Her smile was hard to summon but try she did. She was trained by her mother to smile when out in public after overhearing an unsettling domestic argument between her parents.

'I have a request...' sent a shiver through her, Jace had been aloof, and officious with her and now his humble tone, not quite begging like she wanted to hear, was out of character. His initial representation of himself was a lie, he was far from authentic or honest. To her, he was in a long line of future leaders that had no value to offer education with his slippery tactics, shadowy presence, and false display of humility. She might judge him but there was nothing of value to convince her otherwise.

She felt herself descend into his zone of deception with her ready to please, 'How may I help?'

'It's a request we have of all Brendan Sanchez's teachers. We need to provide the work covered in class to be sent to him while he is away. A file box is on the table outside Mr Alexakis' office and all teachers are to place his work in the box before 3 pm each day.'

The request was a veiled command because the PM's son was away, and he had the right to privilege, his work had to be delivered for every lesson he missed. She had no issue with doing this but wondered if every student in the school had the same respect, or was it for a select few? Dr Horatio's words were coming home to roost — Aurora had unfair connections. She questioned why she was at this school; she could have selected a school that did not have this advantage that she abhorred. But, this was Tempest's decision, and the reason was clear with Junge's kidnapping. Her undercover role would have been easier to conceal if she was in a school unrelated to the crime she was investigating. Here stood Jace Dimakos, perhaps a good man in a personal capacity, but now all she saw was a cog in the giant wheel of deception.

'I will do anything to support all my students.'

She saw him flinch, knowing that he understood that she was fair in her treatment of students — status was not on her roll call.

'Thank you, I'll let you go back to your teaching.'

'Thank you,' Viola stepped away — the chill between them, a growing glacier.

* * *

THAT AFTERNOON she bundled the work for Brendan Sanchez and strolled to the administration block. A large file box labeled *B Sanchez* stood on the table outside Miles' office. She slid the envelope into the box when in that instant the office door opened. Within, she heard the distinct voice of Matthew Soto! She turned and hurried back down the corridor anticipating that he might walk out the door and into her! His words echoed in her head, 'Thank you for all that you're doing.' What was this piece of the puzzle at this stage of their investigation? She felt a hand on her arm and jumped.

It was Vince.

'Hey, Ms Bardo stand still a minute will you before you collide with yourself! What's happened, I couldn't keep pace with you! Has something disturbed you? My American curiosity, sorry! You don't have to say anything that makes you uncomfortable.'

Viola felt immense pressure that she would have to lie to the wonderful, warm, and honest Vince.

'Ladies' room dash, I'm afraid,' with a quick backward glance she hurried out the admin block.

Vince looked at her vanish down the corridor, mystery lady, he whispered to himself.

Viola welcomed the refuge within her classroom with the comfort music instilled.

Maria toddled over to Viola's cottage with dinner for her friend. Her exhausted feet would not stop her from extending some kindness to the lovely Ms Bardo.

'Good to see you back at Aurora, I hope you had a good getaway, although a short one.'

'Thank you, Maria, I did.'

'I figured that the day would have exhausted you, so I brought you some hot mousaka. You can rustle up a salad if you wish.'

'Oh Maria, you are always so thoughtful and kind to me. I have salad leaves, tomatoes and olives to add to your delicious meal.'

'I hope it is delicious, I'll know soon enough when the boarders have digested their meal!' She laughed and squeezed Viola's arm.

'They may be yelling, 'Please Ms Maria, may we have some more?''

'Well, there's plenty more if they do.'

Maria spent half an hour chatting but said nothing about the Sanchez boy or his absence.

VIOLA HAD an anxious time waiting for information on Sebastian's cleaning expedition at Parliament House. It would be tomorrow morning before she had any news. Nights gave them the time and space to meet and discuss the next step in the case. They had to find another way of communicating as time was evaporating. Matthew Soto's presence in Miles' office chewed at her brain.

The web around Junge was complicated — too many high-ranking officials were creating bumps in the investigation. She contemplated that wherever Junge was, he would be feeling abandoned by her — she never reneged on a promise, more so to a child.

Viola knew the pain that followed a broken promise.

* * *

IT WAS during an evening of Christmas window shopping with her mother. She gawked at the heart-shaped jewelry box in the well-lit window casting sparks on the pearl pink necklace, earrings, and bracelet. They lay cradled in a soft heart-shaped sponge. She stared through the window transfixed until her mother's voice broke her joy, 'Do you want that for Christmas?'

'Oh yes please!' Her eyes sparkled as much as the pink pearls. A little girl's joy. Sealed in that moment.

On Christmas morning she rose when all slept in the house. She crept up to the Christmas tree where three gifts lay glittering in red, gold, and green shiny gift wrap. She picked up the gift with her name tag. It was spongy. Perhaps the jewelry box was wrapped with a soft, protective cloth. She was tempted to rip it open, but did not want to incur her mother's anger for what would end her already miserable holiday season.

Her mother waltzed downstairs at 7:30 am dressed in a red and green dress with large wooden Christmas tree earrings bouncing just above her shoulders. Her rush of tight curls pinned atop her head.

'Ah, thought you would get in before Santa?' Her mother laughed.

'I woke up early and peeked.'

'We must shower first and be fresh before we open the presents.'

Viola was confused why her mother spoke of *we* when she was already fresh and sparkling for Christmas Day. Their family was never an, *us*, or *we* family with her parent's dissension, she wanted her family to be together, but that choice was not hers.

With fresh smelling hands she opened her present and was crushed. Her present, in the middle of an African summer, was a pair of woolen gloves, a hat, and a scarf.

'Don't you just love it? My friend Tembi bought it for me when she was on vacation in England.'

'It's lovely,' she said trying to swallow the tears stinging her eyes. She had to accept it, and remain silent, she knew disappointment was unacceptable when there were many starving children in the world. Ingratitude was unacceptable in her mother's house. And so, the pink pearls cradled in a heart-shaped box lingered in the background of her childhood winters — waiting for some other child.

Her ringing phone caught her attention. The anxious voice on the other end sounded familiar.

'HELLO... hello,... Ms Bardo... is that you?'

'Yes, it is Viola Bardo, who is this?'

'It's Bernice Soto, have you heard from Matthew? I am worried, he has not returned home today as he does, and he's not answering his phone.'

What hit Viola in the head was that her caller was Bernice *Soto*, confirming without a doubt that she was Matthew's relative!

'Bernice, where are you calling from? No, I've had no word from Matthew. I went to the house and, you all had left.'

Silence

'Bernice?'

'I've rattled on too much, sorry to have troubled you, Ms Bardo, but if you hear from Matthew, please tell him to call me, please.'

She hung up.

SLEEP WAS a remote possibility that night as question after question filled her mind. Where was Matthew Soto? Why was he in Miles' office? Where was Junge?

Finding Junge was paramount. She knew the love and security of being in her father's home.

17

T wo days

Viola took a half day off from Aurora. She had many things to discuss with Sebastian to segment what needed urgent attention. News of Matthew's situation left her anguished for Junge's safety. She trusted that the child would be safe and loved in Matthew's care. What else did a six-year-old need?

She arrived at Sebastian's apartment at 1:30 pm.

He had an interesting night as assistant head cleaner at Parliament House.

'The team has six people, all have been with the company for over three years. There was nothing much I could show them so that gave me time to snoop as I do! And snoop I did in the upstairs offices.' His words flowed at a speed faster than his usual pace, his left foot tapped in agitation on the kitchen tiles. Viola wondered whether it was excitement at having discovered something, or perhaps exhaustion from sleep deprivation?

She leaned forward when his pace slowed down, and his tone softened.

'I ventured past the end of the last corridor and noticed the staff had missed an office tucked under a stairway. I had a look — boy am I glad I did!'

'Come on, don't leave me hanging.'

'There was someone in the office on the telephone, or so I thought. It was ten minutes after midnight, I was eager to know who was working at this hour in a hidden office.'

'Who was it, Sebastian? I haven't had any sugar today so don't keep me in suspense. Who knows what might have happened to you for taking such a risk? And on your own!' She tried to keep a serious face, but Sebastian's dramatic, shocked expression tickled her.

Part of her speculated if it was Miles Alexakis, as he had connections with Parliament House. It could be Matthew Soto. He was missing.

'Thing is the voice was not on the telephone because I heard another voice respond to the first voice. I crept up to the ajar door and lo and behold saw the Prime Minister but not the person he was conversing with. He was scratching his head in vigorous agitation, and get this, the unseen speaker had a strong German accent!'

'The Ambassador?' Viola exclaimed. 'Are you sure about that?'

'Who else could it be? My gut tells me these two are in cahoots over regaining the boy and got rid of Matthew Soto.'

'Do you mean killed him?'

'Well, that's one possibility but they could have moved him to another location.'

'It's speculation if you did not see the man with the German accent and it's imperative that we inform Tempest.' Viola sensed that Tempest already knew the details.

'Good afternoon team!' Tempest cooed across the airwaves.

'It's good to have you both together on a weekday, quite a treat. But I foresee that you both are in for a long night.' She continued until she had finished her revelations while ignoring Sebastian's need to interrupt her.

'Bernice Soto is Matthew's stepmother, his birth mother died when his sister was born. His father married Bernice, who at the time was their neighbor. But, it gets complicated...'

Silence from the team as Viola and Sebastian considered what more could add complications to the complexity they already faced.

'Bernice's boyfriend was a German migrant living in the United States but wait for it... she is the mother of the German Ambassador — her parents gave her baby up for adoption because family law decreed an intolerance to having an unwed mother in their home. The Ambassador's father was a German soldier. He had no clue that she was his mother.'

'Wow!' Viola said and kept silent to digest it all. Then she added, 'This means I'm right about Matthew. If the child's biological grandmother is supporting Matthew in illegally harboring Junge, then surely he does not intend to harm the boy. Right? I did not expect to hear that Bernice was not biologically related to Matthew. I saw a resemblance.'

'But, what if she is in it with him, out of fear? If anyone knows Matthew Soto well, it would be Bernice because she raised him.'

'Sorry Sebastian, I do not see Matthew as that guy, my gut is right on this.'

'I love it team, agree to disagree because in that is the capacity to unravel this case.'

'But,' Sebastian broke in, 'why are we returning the child if his grandmother has him?'

'Fair point. All should make sense soon. I have the details of where Junge and Bernice are and need you both to go there on a stakeout tonight. I need answers on how we will remove the child from the cottage where they are being held. He must be returned to the Ambassador. Remember, we are working for him and he does not know you, so that helps us delve deeper into why this situation occurred.' On that note she rattled off the location and switched off her device.

Viola stared at the wall, segmenting all that she had heard. Sebastian looked up the location Tempest provided for their stake out.

'Snap out of it, Viola, we have to think up a course of action right away. Junge and Bernice are a little out of Athens central, so we should build in some travel time to get there and back. I have to call the cleaning company and say I need a sick day, something I've never done in my life with just the second day on the job!'

'Yeah, I can't take another day's leave with today's half day off. I have to get back to Aurora in the morning.'

'Carry a set of clothes to change on the way back to Athens to allow you to save time getting to your class.'

'Change in the car?' Viola shook her head.

'We must leave as soon as it's dark to avoid being seen heading that way. Hopefully, no tourists are there, that distance away from Athens. I'll top up the fuel tank and buy some supplies to sustain us for the night. We must charge our devices before we set out.'

Viola's hand slid into her handbag — she had to have some peanut brittle for the expected tense night ahead. All she had, was two little pieces, crushed inside a plastic zip-lock pouch.

'We should carry water, and I'll fill up the thermos with coffee.'

'Great, I'll be back soon, grab whatever you can to make it a little less uncomfortable tonight.'

The situation they were in appeared to be a domestic arrangement to the unknowing eye, of a couple heading out on an adventure. She searched the kitchen cupboard, no thermos!

How could Sebastian think he had one? She called him. He said he would pick up one from the store around the corner from his apartment. It was imperative that he try somewhere else to avoid leaving any tracks if the situation got out of hand that night. Viola tossed whatever she could find into the cooler bag, cheese, olives, bread rolls. That should sustain them with coffee for the night.

Sebastian returned laden with groceries for a large family. He threw her a bag, 'Catch!'

She grabbed the bag mid-air. It was a bag of peanut brittle!

'Where did you find this? Thank you!' She could have hugged him in that moment but maintained her officious attitude. A level head was needed for the mission ahead.

'In a dark corner at the all-night supermarket, I hope it's within the edible date!'

'I don't care, when I need this sugar hit, I need it!'

'Junkie!'

Sebastian grabbed two hooded jackets and reached into the cupboard for his gun.

Viola froze, she never resorted to firearms, using only her wit to get her through confrontational situations.

'Please, do you need to take that?'

'Just a precautionary measure.'

'Tempest did not issue any warnings that we were going into dangerous territory that warranted the use of firearms.'

Lourenço Marques left her with a scarred memory of gun-toting Frelimo terrorists at the border. The move to Australia was for a gun free lifestyle.

With their food supplies, hooded jackets, binoculars, and Sebastian's concealed firearm, they slipped out of the apartment and crawled out of Athens.

18

The derelict, ramshackle farmhouse skulked under a black night sky, haunting, and disturbing.

Sebastian parked the car behind a clump of lifeless trees.

'Here are the keys, should we need to depart in haste?'

'I might not have told you, but I don't...'

Her whisper went unheard in the chilly breeze rustling through the trees as he hurried her out the car. They stepped out and slouched towards the building — hunting beasts on the prowl. Sebastian's gun was at the ready. The light in a downstairs window of the building was dull. It was 9:30 pm. Something small, or crouching, moved in and out of the window frame.

'Could that be Junge?'

'At this hour? I doubt it.'

'It's not a normal situation so he might well be awake.'

'Let's stop here to see if there is more movement to get a sense of who is inside.'

They lay low for half an hour but nothing moved inside the ghostly cottage.

Then almost as if they had willed her, Bernice Soto came to the window, looked out, left to right, scanning, searching. Viola had the urge to wave or call out, but reason cautioned safety. Aunt Lorenza taught her that patience was a necessary virtue, something she clung to in her life decisions. Soon a slim male figure joined her at the window, and she pushed him out of view.

A gut instinct convinced Viola that the boys, Brendan and Junge, were in the house. Apart from Bernice's searching look, nothing untoward appeared to be happening. Why were they here, gnawed at Viola?

'We need to get closer to the house, it's difficult to discern the mood of the occupants from this distance, the light is faint inside the house,' Sebastian whispered.

A shed stood to the left of the main building with a cluster of tall trees swaying as the breeze gained momentum.

'We should take shelter behind the shed.'

'Are you expecting a hail of bullets, it's awfully quiet.'

'Not a time for such jokes, I know you oppose firearms, but it's our safety that matters. What's that? Did you hear that?'

'Hurry across to the back of the shed, a car is approaching, I saw a beam of light...'

They crawled on all fours to the back of the shed as the dark sedan came to a halt. The driver switched off the lights, but nobody alighted from the vehicle. Viola pondered whether it was the same dark vehicle she saw on its menacing cruise past Soto's house.

She sucked in her breath when the car lights turned on again and the car crept closer to the building shining its headlights onto the verandah. An old swing seat creaked and groaned like someone had sat on it a minute ago.

'What the hell?' Sebastian hissed.

Questions burned on why this abandoned building lay forgotten on the outskirts of a busy cosmopolitan metropolis. The car lights turned off again and the driver-side door opened. A tall, chunky figure stepped out. At first it was difficult to determine gender. Long, curly hair framed the head. When the person walked to the passenger door, it was clear it was a man from the square shape, and gait.

He yanked someone from the passenger seat. Viola knew the figure — Matthew Soto! The bulky driver then dragged someone out the backseat, shoved a gun into his back and pushed him and Soto forward to walk towards the building.

'Who are these people, the driver and the passenger are unknowns to me.'

'Once we get closer, fingers crossed, we might have an idea,' Sebastian clenched his teeth, 'we have to creep closer to the house once they get inside.'

The moon grew shadowy stealing the little light they had, and Sebastian caught Viola's silhouette with her finger to her lips. The cottage door opened.

In the faint light of the doorway Viola saw Junge lunge at Soto and grab him around the legs. The burly driver shoved the boy away. Junge looked behind Soto and cried out, 'Papa!'

Viola and Sebastian whispered instantaneously, 'The Ambassador...'

The door shut.

Sebastian stood up, then dived back onto the ground when the door opened again. The driver looked out, shone his torch-light across the yard, an invasive surveillance beam searching for a target. Viola inhaled the dry dust — she was in a full eagle spread on the ground, Sebastian lay beside her in the same position. The light circled the shed before the door shut again.

'Phew! I was ready to make a run for it!'

This was the first time since they met that Viola heard this level of tension in Sebastian's voice. He dashed across the front yard up to the side of the building, and covered Viola with the gun as she made a dash across but stopped midway when a dry twig cracked under her foot — then she darted across to Sebastian.

They slunk close to the building, there were no trees on the periphery of the house to offer them seclusion. She yanked off her hoop earrings that never left her ears and shoved them in her jacket pocket.

Sebastian crawled up to the window that Bernice had peered through. It was silent in the house until Junge's ear shattering cry, 'Onkel Matt, onkel!'

Viola's heart lurched — she crawled up beside Sebastian, he held her down from wanting to look through the window. He crouched at the side of the door from where the voices within where audible. The woman's voice begged, 'Please put the gun away, Matthew will cause no harm, I promise. He values the boy's and my safety.'

'Shut up! Or I will shoot you first!' The gunmen yelled — his accent was unmistakably American. The puzzle pieces fell away as the unknown confronted Viola and Sebastian.

Then Viola recognized Brendan's voice, 'Please call my father for whatever you want, but please don't hurt us.' A scuffling sound had both concerned for Brendan's safety.

'You bloody rich politician's kids, is that all you care about — money? Speak again and a bullet goes through your indulgent, spoilt head, you hear me!'

Brendan was silent.

There was no movement or sound for twenty minutes until the gunman's harsh voice growled at Bernice, 'Hey lady, make me a pot of strong coffee.'

Bernice's muffled voice, heavy with crying muttered, 'I don't think we have enough milk for a pot of coffee.'

'I don't drink black coffee. Here take these keys and go to

the car, there's a box of milk in the boot and some soft drinks, bring them in!'

'I can't carry it on my own, may I take Brendan with me?' Her voice sounded like that of a child asking for a favor.

This enraged the gunman. He pulled Matthew Soto to his feet and placed the gun on his left temple. A gasp from inside echoed to Viola outside.

'Do you think I'm stupid! Make two trips and don't try any funny business!'

Sebastian was back at the window, he looked down a passage. He saw Matthew Soto's lowered head with his eyes riveted to the floor, afraid to lift them for fear he would put Bernice at risk.

She picked up the keys and opened the door, Viola had moved to the side of the cottage, and plastered herself against the wall. She pulled the hood over her head — this was not the time for Bernice to see her. Sebastian crept behind Bernice, he placed a hand on her mouth and whispered in her ear, 'Do not make a sound. I'm here to help, do as you are told.' Her saucer eyes welled up, she nodded and walked to the car. She had left the cottage door wide open. Sebastian was about to step inside and reconsidered — he needed to be there while Bernice was outside.

She returned to the cottage with the milk searching for a glimpse of who spoke to her and then picked up the soft drinks and shut the door. Viola peered in through the window and saw nothing but the back of Matthew's head, she slipped back to the side of the house.

The other man who was silent, now begged, 'Please let the children go, please.' His German accent was distinct.

That was the switch that sent the gunman into an angry spiral.

'You, worried about the safety of the children is a joke! You never cared for your son from the day he was born! What a bloody hypocrite!'

Viola and Sebastian felt the aggression in his voice. They knew that the mood had shifted to the next level of danger, and had to be prepared for anything. When agitation crept in, the gunman dropped his elusiveness by conveying that he knew the Ambassador well — now the question was how did he fit into the puzzle because nothing made sense if he held Matthew hostage? Viola crept back onto the verandah.

The gunman stepped to the window. Sebastian dived onto the ground, flat in the dirt. The gunman leered out the window and returned to where Matthew, Bernice, the Ambassador, and the boys were sitting.

THE NIGHT WAS LONG.

Out in a place where nobody dared venture, Viola and Sebastian waited for the next move.

19

W aiting... and waiting...

10:30 pm

THE STILLNESS around the abandoned building grew eerier with each hour and the intensity of the rising chill stung their cheeks. Wasted, freshly brewed coffee, abandoned in the car hidden in the thickness between a cluster of trees.

Viola pulled her jacket up to her lips. Her bad teeth were victims of the increasing chill — pain shot up to her temples assaulting her with every open-mouthed inhalation. She tucked her hands into her pockets. The toothache did not deter her — how she wished she had stashed the pack of peanut brittle in her jacket pocket. It was Sebastian's jacket, and gooey caramel, lining his pocket, was not a memory she wanted to imprint. He lay silent on the ground beside her.

Bats flapped overhead agitated by the wind.

'I'm going to the shed — call of nature...'

'Go to the side of the cottage, you're a man, anywhere is fine for you.'

'I'm trying to be the gentleman, here, but if you're happy, your suggestion it shall be.'

'No time now, for gallantry sir!'

'Glad you still have a sense of humor.'

'Barely, my mouth might freeze into a locked jaw soon if this cold gets worse.'

He jumped up in desperation, kept close against the wall, and disappeared around the corner. She felt the iciness increase with the vacant spot Sebastian left. He was back sooner than he left.

'Washed your hands?' she whispered.

'I wish we had that five star luxury here! Any movement?'

'No, just yours. We might have to leave if nothing gives tonight.'

'I'm going into the house through that verandah window. You keep watch here and alert me with a quick text message, hopefully the phone vibrating in my pocket should attract my attention.'

'Be careful...'

Sebastian slipped onto the verandah, lifted the wooden window frame. It threatened to slip back down with the aged, brittle wood offering no secure grip to hold it up. He wedged the side with a paper napkin he had slipped into his pocket before they left the apartment. He tumbled into the cottage.

Viola heaved a deep sigh and realized she had to get closer to hear what might emerge from the cottage. The howling wind blocked out sounds that she needed to hear should Sebastian require urgent back-up inside.

She heard heavy breathing and jumped out of her skin. It came from her listening device. Sebastian had turned on his device to allow her to hear the movements inside. He must have been crawling on the floor — there was a swishing sound which might have been his pants dragging across a dusty floor. His breathing sounded like he was right beside her — one device, a watch, could have been near his mouth to sound so close. She visualized him crawling with his head low on his arms.

Her phone vibrated in her pants pocket, she yanked it out. A message from Sebastian read, *All asleep here. Stay there until I tell you to move inside.*

She replied, *OK.* Her phone battery was on half-life, she had to keep her phone switched off to preserve it for urgent matters. Loneliness crept over her with Sebastian inside, she felt abandoned with him gone and her phone turned off.

Then without an inkling rain gushed down. Within seconds she was drenched to the skin. Damn Sebastian he got out just in time. She ran up to the verandah and flopped close to the window that he disappeared through.

Viola hummed an old tune in her head to stop her craving for a cup of coffee and her sweet anti-stress treat. If she was not covering Sebastian's back, she would dash to the car, the keys were in her pocket.

A gut-wrenching wail passed under the front door of the building. It was Junge — Viola pressed her ear against the door when a raised male voice cut through the gushing rain.

'Shut up! Stop the boy now!'

'He is exhausted, this is a strange set-up for him. He'll settle soon.' She heard Matthew Soto's pleading voice. Junge wailed for a full five minutes, coughing in between — heavy footsteps stomped on the old wooden floors.

The dusty curtains rose and floated out the window until it was a drenched lifeless sodden mess. Viola had the urge to jump in through the window, but the risk was too great. Everybody inside was awake.

Sebastian got in undetected and hid in the hallway

cupboard to be close to where everyone had gathered. He needed to hear what the gunman was planning. Was he a legitimate driver or posing as one?

The dank odor of mold in the damp cupboard clung to his clothes choking him. He wondered how old the building was and whether anybody owned the property. He tried to send Viola a message again, but she was offline. A message to Tempest was necessary now that he was in a dangerous situation.

THE RAIN STOPPED with the same abruptness with which it began. Viola reached for her phone, turned in on to check if Sebastian had made contact again. All he said was, *no change.*

The faint light from her phone was useless in this blackness. Then a glint of light appeared, reflected on the window, growing closer, sending Viola into a palpitating twitch. She glanced in the shed's direction — a refuge from whatever was approaching. When she looked behind her, there was no light. She blinked. Her mother's advancing glaucoma made her think she had fallen prey to the same in this anxious moment. Her unremitting rational mind said that it was a passing car, her active imagination whispered with a croak that someone was right there before her.

Her worst nightmare was a loud bang as the decrepit window frame shut!

Sebastian was trapped inside. He had no way out!

She bent as low as possible and scurried behind the shed. Stillness again, no wind, no rain and yet the window slammed shut. She reached for her phone, concealing the lit screen under her jacket sleeve. It was 11:45 pm. For fifteen minutes she sat on her haunches, her legs were numb with cold and a lack of circulation. She steadied herself on the side of the shed and pulled her body to a standing position to get the blood pumping in her legs, ready to sprint out of there. As she wriggled her legs around, a shattering gunshot penetrated the night air and echoed in the stillness around her.

The front door of the cottage flung open!

A figure that appeared male under this black night, carried a child and darted out the building— then a lean figure ran out behind him. Instinct told Viola it was Sebastian carrying Junge with Brendan following close on his heels. She heard Sebastian call out, 'Come on! Get out!' He turned his head in the direction of the shed as he hurried to the car, trying to keep upright with the boy in his arms. This was a call to her. One she could not heed. Both children knew her. That would compromise the entire case and her exchange position at Aurora. Sebastian opened the back door of the vehicle that Matthew arrived in. He gently placed Junge in Brendan's arms, looked again in the direction of the shed, shut the door, and got into the driver's seat.

All three sped away in search of safety. She saw the rear lights disappear into the night.

She was alone with nowhere to hide.

Headlights lit up from the field in front of the house.

The elusive vehicle reappeared!

How much did the occupants see? Did they know she was behind the shed? Viola bobbed up and down on her feet preparing for a quick flight out of there. The vehicle spun around and followed Sebastian.

THE DRIVER WALKED out the door with Bernice and Matthew in front of him. His gun prodded their backs. Mesmerized by this vision, her gaze diverted from another vehicle that pulled up outside the cottage, the driver shoved Bernice and Matthew in and jumped in with them. The vehicle raced away.

The gunman was not a lone operator.

She was tired and thirsty.

The front door was open, and a faint glow framed the doorway.

It was time for her to investigate the inside of the building. Junge and Brendan were in safe hands — she hoped.

2 0

She walked down the winding passageway. A wavering light cast dim dancing shadows onto the floor. The room at the end of the passageway had a large dining table with couches lined against the rear right wall. An oil lamp stood in its swan song, falling and rising, unable to brighten the room. Viola tripped over something and fell onto the table sending the oil lamp crashing onto its brittle tinder-dry top. It lit up the table in an instant. Then in that moment of brilliant light she saw trousered legs and black glossy shoes, jutting out from under the table. She reached to drag the person out when the couches caught alight spreading rapidly to the left wall. This inner room had no windows. She scurried back down the corridor towards the front door, revving her flailing energy as fire snaked down the passage behind her.

Viola dived off the verandah and landed headlong in a muddy puddle. She stood up and bolted for the gate and kept running in the direction where Sebastian had parked the car among the tall conifers.

The dark sky now a vermilion blaze behind her urged her to hasten her step.

After a few circles in the wrong direction she found the car, grabbed the keys that Sebastian had the foresight to entrust in her safekeeping, She sat back in the driver's seat. What good was it having the keys? It had been over ten years since she had last driven a car — her nerves had shut out the skills she knew so well. Her phone lit up on her lap. A message from Sebastian yelled, *GET OUT OF THERE ASAP. Police are on their way.*

She replied, *OMG! Fire at the cottage.*

Her phone pinged again, *GET OUT NOW.*

Viola closed her eyes — she had to do this. There was no way of getting out of here on foot. She shut her eyes summoning her memory to guide her, and the gods to thaw her fear of the ghastly time that put an end to her driving. The dreaded day a woman ran onto the freeway when she was traveling at 100 km. Only later in the emergency room after the ambulance picked up the woman who had multiple injuries from the impact, did Viola know that she was running away from an enraged partner who was chasing her with a knife. She scaled the fence that backed up onto the freeway and ran across as Viola's car sped past. She swerved to avoid hitting the woman — but the back, right end of the car sent the woman hurtling into a ditch. Viola had a broken wrist and whiplash. The woman who appeared out of nowhere haunted her for many years. She never forgave herself and no amount of counseling gave her the courage to drive again. The what ifs had her in a high state of anxiety for a long time... what if ...the woman had died... what if... she could never walk again... what if... she was pregnant... what if...?

She called upon her former self when she was a confident driver, careful, always cautious. Her mother taunted her about taking an eternity at the stop sign, waiting for the whole city to pass before she crossed the intersection. With a quick flick she turned the key in the ignition and broke into a cold sweat. She clutched the steering wheel, closed her eyes, and visualized the steps as she did as a little girl instructing her father to turn off the indicator, pull up the hand brake and switch off the car. In parrot fashion she memorized the steps of keeping a car on the road. She followed through on the steps but hit the accelerator too hard almost sending the car into a tree — she swerved and steadied her nerves. This time she started the car and pressed the accelerator with a light foot. The car hesitated forward — she stopped, turned on her cell phone and set off again, she needed her GPS to get her back to Aurora Academy. It was 1:45 am on the car clock. She slipped across the landscape and soon her phone was dead. A back-up phone was in a bag in the car's trunk. She pulled up and rifled through the glove box and found a car charger which she hooked up to bring her battery back to life. She mulled over how she would get into the school grounds undetected and decided that parking a few streets away was her only option. Her phone interrupted her thoughts and her GPS connection. It was Sebastian. She pulled over for the third time and returned his call. Multitasking while driving was not a skill after a decade of fear.

'Where are you? I've been trying to call you, there was no signal.'

'Driving towards Aurora,' she wanted to tell him to come and get her, that she had not driven a car in almost ten years...

'Keep to the main road if your GPS cuts off, it's a straight run until you get to the vicinity near the school and you know the rest from there.'

'Where are the boys?'

'Safe in police custody, I had to do that to avoid being implicated in the kidnapping. Don't worry, they're fine. Brendan Sanchez is some kid!' before he could elaborate Viola piped in, 'Did he do something wrong?'

'Far from it, he was a godsend in helping me with Junge, Brendan is a mature lad for his age, a well-bred fellow for sure.'

'Well, his father is the Prime Minister.'

. . .

VIOLA ARRIVED at Aurora around 3 am, and parked Sebastian's car a street away from the main gate and sprinted towards the school. George was not on duty that night so she would have to sneak in to avoid being detected. She duck waddled past the gatehouse, then hunched over and ran across to the teachers' residence. She reached into her pocket for her cottage key. It was not there! It was in the bag in the car. Her verandah window was ajar, she was about to force it open when a torch-light beamed down the footpath towards her cottage. She lay flat on the floor behind the potted palm, holding her breath, praying for the moment to pass. The crunching footsteps stopped in front of her door, the torchlight flashed across the verandah, then she heard departing footsteps. She scaled in through the window grazing her knees on the windowsill. A call to Sebastian was urgent. The relief in his voice was what she needed.

'Viola! Thank god you're back at Aurora. What took you so long? I feared that you might have taken a wrong turn.'

'Long story, but I'm here now.'

'Here's a quick heads-up on the boys, I left them outside the police station with a note and parked close by to make sure they got in, and I left the car there to avoid any tracking back to me.'

'They are in safe hands, I hope. I will take a half day's leave, depending on Miles' mood, and see you at the apartment after midday.'

'What did you say about the fire, last night?'

'There was a man on the floor, I tripped over him and that set the oil lamp off on its destructive journey. I don't know if I have burned the building to the ground.'

'Dear god! That was the Ambassador, Junge's father. I

wonder if he's dead.' As any typical agent, he focused on the case, and offered no sympathy for her guilt.

'There's nothing we can do now, Sebastian. I'm not sure how this will sit with Tempest, that we don't have the boy.'

'We'll leave that for tomorrow although I suspect she might already know.'

AFTER A RESTLESS TWO hours lying in bed staring at the ceiling, Viola poured herself a strong cup of coffee and headed to the admin block to see Miles.

Sitting behind Miles' desk was Jace Dimakos with a smug look etched across his face.

'Good morning, Ms Bardo, what brings you to me this early in the morning?'

Brings you to *me*, what a pompous idiot!

'Sorry to barge in without an appointment, I need to take a half day's leave today.'

'Everything OK, Ms Bardo? Yes, that should be in order, let Mr Alexakis' PA know so she can arrange cover for you this afternoon.

'Yes, all good, thanks,' and she added before he had time to think, 'I have to see my dentist this afternoon, I cracked a tooth and have excruciating pain.'

'Best you get it done soon. Will that be all this morning?'

'Yes thank you, Mr Dimakos.' The formality seemed appropriate to his lord of the manor attitude. Each time she encountered Jace Dimakos he was more insufferable than the last, she was glad to get away from him. She had to cover her dentist tracks and rang Sebastian to book her an appointment with Dr Horatio. Her suspicions of Jace had her believing he would track her phone usage and listen in to her calls.

By the time she was ready to leave that afternoon she had a 3:30 pm appointment booked with Dr Horatio. She expected to see Brendan in class that morning, but the turmoil of the night before would have left him stressed and anxious. A quick trip to the library after her meeting with Jace was not as she expected. The librarian was poring over the daily newspaper reading out an article to an attentive group of three teachers.

Viola apologized for barging in and saw the blaring headlines.

German Ambassador in Critical Condition.

A photograph of the burning building under the headline made Viola lightheaded. The librarian saw her lean against the desk to steady herself.

'Are you not feeling well, Ms Bardo?'

'No, no, I am well thanks, what's this that you're reading?'

'Oh terrible business at an abandoned building, outside the city. It's known as the ghost cottage to some. The visiting Ambassador was here the day before this awful news. What a wonderful talk he gave the assembly. It's just shocking reading this.' She pushed the newspaper towards Viola and the three teachers walked away, lost in their private thoughts on the matter.

The last paragraph in the article gnawed at her.

Police are keen to track the movements at the abandoned building on that fateful night.

Junge and Brendan had no mention in the article. Political immunity, perhaps, protected children of high-ranking officials.

What if the Ambassador did not make it through this ordeal? What would happen to Junge? If the Ambassador survived would he connect Sebastian to the events that night?

The question that weighted on her mind was whether Sebastian had anything to do with the shooting?

Viola arrived at Dr Horatio's rooms around three fifteen that afternoon.

Her agitation carved a scowl across her face. This contrived appointment made her uncomfortable. It could lead to anything, unheard information on the case, more dental work than she needed, temporary paralysis of her face and the warning to stay off the peanut brittle!

Two women were ahead of her in the queue in the waiting room. She knew appointment times at any good dentist could be anywhere from twenty to thirty minutes off schedule in any country in any part of the world! The television news ran with the sound muted and sub-titles rolling through. A replay on the fire at the cottage revealed the status of the Ambassador's condition. The red-haired woman to Viola's left looked at the woman next to her and said, 'Terrible business, the government should demolish abandoned buildings, not leave them vacant. It encourages sordid activities.'

The other woman replied with Viola straining to hear her, 'Perhaps we should not have private schools — too much privilege and politics and look at what happens. They should get down to the business of teaching and not flaunting overseas politicians for fame. In my day it was studying and gaining sporting and artistic skills — nothing more, and the world was a better place for it.'

All the red-haired woman did was nod in agreement, and mutter, 'Sad, it is sad.'

On that note Dr Horatio stepped out the door with his cheerful grin and escorted Viola into his room.

'Back so soon? How can I help you?'

'Nothing major this time, just a general clean is all today, thanks. Too much coffee seems to stain my teeth.'

'Whitening toothpaste should do the trick. Simple!'

She knew that, she used it but needed to fill in some idle talk. Risking appearing stupid, was part of her required skills as a vigilante investigator when cracking the lid on truth. She might never see Dr Horatio again in her life, yet she smarted at his mocking tone and the thought of the label he would tack on her.

Rob Dwyer recommended her as an intelligent, intuitive and accomplished music teacher. That meant nothing in a foreign country, she had to earn her colors with colleagues, leaders, and the community. With her mouth wide open in the most unbecoming contorted ahh grimace she thought about the many times she would have to reinvent herself as a migrant seeking a new life, or in her case many lives in foreign places. It was almost as if Dr Horatio had read her thoughts.

'How are things at Aurora Academy? Crikey, that business with the foreign Ambassador is a shocker! He visited the school the day before this nasty situation. What did you make of him?' He paused to hear her response.

It was awkward to speak with her overstretched jaw and she was irritated by his prying questions. After all she did not ask him for an airing of the board of dentists dirty linen! But he expected an answer, he stopped working on her teeth, placed his cleaning utensils down, determined to be privy to a juicy bit of gossip.

'I was away for a few days, so I missed seeing him.'

Thankfully, she did not have to tell a white lie nor provide a detailed rendition of what she thought of the Ambassador.

She closed her eyes and willed him to proceed without further, unrelated to the job, questions. It was no wonder that appointments spilled over the allotted time. He had no intention of stopping what was on his mind.

'It has been quiet on the Aurora front in recent days. I remember a few years back some scandalous business went on at the school. Many teachers were made redundant. All surreptitiously done, no information leaked, a sealed vault, I tell you. Not even the media knew, or perhaps they were blocked from knowing. Alexakis is the longest standing member of staff there.'

She was grateful for her incapacitated mouth, or she would have declared him incorrect. Maria was the longest standing member of staff at Aurora. This small-town gossip was something she had not anticipated prior to arriving here. He droned on that the school might get a poor rap from the newspaper on the Ambassador's current condition. Viola nodded throughout his ramblings, and jumped up, relieved when the ordeal was over. As much as she relied on information to resolve a case, idle chatter annoyed her the most. 'Great to see you again, I hope all goes well for you at Aurora and your teeth!' He guffawed from behind his mask. How he knew the intricacies of Aurora's inside story bothered her, she was silent on matters regarding the case. Tempest arranged her first dental appointment, confirming he had an unspoken connection with her. How many players were there in Tempest's web?

SEBASTIAN MET her outside his apartment, needing some air

and a bit of a walk. She wanted to be indoors away from prying eyes.

He was pensive, not his usual jovial self.

'We have to crack this soon. Tempest is not happy with how things have turned out. She expects us to come up with the goods ASAP.'

'Why is she upset if Junge is safe? Please don't refer to him as *goods*. You should not say that to a school-teacher, or anyone.'

Her protective, maternal, teacher instinct was the hallmark of her personality.

'I'm so sorry that is not what I meant at all. I would never refer to the child that way.' He blubbered, struggling with how things went awry at the shoot-out at the cottage, and that he had abandoned her. Her sensitive side kicked in, and his despair had to be lifted so she suggested they go back to his apartment to work on a new strategy.

'We both need a glass of wine. I have slept little and suspect the same for you.'

'I am exhausted so I don't think wine will be good for my head.'

'I want to hear the details of what happened once you entered the cottage. If you don't mind, I need to kick off my shoes first before I hear it all.'

He managed a faint smile for the first time since she arrived, her laid-back attitude was rare. The uptight Viola he first met was now a little chilled in his company.

THE NIGHT UNFOLDED like she was in the building with him. Sebastian spared no details. He was a visual storyteller, painting the events in florid details.

The silence broke when Junge began crying — it agitated the gunman who paced like a caged bear. Sebastian believed that he was coming down from an amphetamine high. His eyes bulged and the veins in his neck were taut and ready to burst. Things grew increasingly tense from that moment. Matthew Soto appealed for calm to help Junge settle. He tried reasoning that the situation was something the boy had never encountered before. The gunman scoffed saying the kidnapping happened a while ago, so this should be bearable for him. There was no point talking to a junkie who could only see the world through his own highs and lows. There was a brief period of quiet until the Ambassador walked towards Junge — that's when the berserk gunman fired, hitting the Ambassador in the chest. He fell like a dried wattle. The bullet missed the child by inches. Somehow the gunman seemed more surprised than any of the others. He knelt beside the Ambassador saying something incoherent in German. This was Sebastian's opportunity to seize the moment of escape. Brendan looked at him and somehow picked up the cue to run. He snatched Junge off the floor and ran out the building with Brendan following close behind him. At this point Viola wanted to know why the gunman did not chase after them to stop them from escaping.

'I think it was the first time he had ever fired a gun. He froze in a trance when the Ambassador hit the ground. This confirmed that he was coming down from some narcotic substance — he looked exhausted and would have had a muzzy, sore head for sure.'

Viola questioned why Matthew and Bernice did not run out with him. They were at the back end of the room, on the opposite side of the large conference table. That would have made it difficult and risky for them to pass the gunman without a crazed attack from him. This could have prevented them leaving.

Viola sighed, 'I hope the boys are safe and well. Nothing must happen to them although the Ambassador's son is our concern.' Her big, soft, generous heart warmed him. How he wished he could have been a student in her class. His teachers were strict, no play allowed, and no opinions permitted. His father put him in the military academy, that's where he learned all his investigative and defence skills, but now he could not put them to use.

'I will never rest until Junge is in the care of his father as Tempest requested. Trust me on this.'

She looked at him and her heart melted, he could so easily be her little brother playing the big brother. She longed for that kinship as a child. Between an artist father and literary mother, she was, for most of her early childhood, left to her own devices.

Sebastian turned on the television news for an update. Within seconds, breaking news announced in an eye-catching flashing footnote that the Ambassador was in a critical condition and on life support.

'Just what I hoped would not happen,' Viola groaned covering her face with her hands.

Sebastian called Tempest to discuss restructuring their plans. Viola cleared away the wine glasses. Tempest had strict rules about alcohol and working hours. She ran a tight, professional task force. A vegan lifestyle kept her alert. That was as much that Viola knew about her. She slipped that in during one of their earlier conversations but now she was a shut book. They waited with nervous energy for her usual greeting.

'Viola, Sebastian,' is all they heard in Tempest's clipped tone. Her displeasure was clear. She was ready to hang someone out to dry.

'Good evening, Tempest,' they both muttered without their usual lyrical greeting.

'I have a few things that need clarifying before I proceed with the meeting on where this investigation should be going.'

No response...

'First, if you're on a team, that's what you are, right? No solo acts unless agreed. Got that Sebastian?'

He sat bolt upright, 'Yes Tempest.'

'Are you aware of what I refer to regarding the night in question?'

Sebastian felt the pressure. He was in the dock facing the judge, prosecutor, and the jury. He had to respond.

'Yes, I should not have left Viola on her own in a dangerous situation at the building.'

'Bingo!'

'The situation got out of hand once the Ambassador was down, and I instinctively felt Junge was my priority.'

'Say that again.'

Sebastian hesitated, his body stiffened, cold from this open dressing down. Viola's eyes moved to the stain on the carpet.

'Your priority includes all people I place on a team. The same applies to Viola and whoever is on Team Tempest, and that includes the German Ambassador. He is our client, he put us on this investigation. Got it?'

Sebastian's shame and regret were loaded in his morose tone, 'A hundred percent, madam.'

She ignored his response and addressed Viola who at this stage was trembling expecting to be chastised for something.

'How are you Viola after that ordeal of being abandoned by your team-mate here?'

Her terseness silenced Viola. It was an awkward situation to be in and not for a moment did she believe that Sebastian abandoned her that night.

'I'm okay, thank you. I got away.'

'By Divine Grace!'

Viola blinked, unsure if she heard Tempest correctly. Did Tempest know she could not drive? Or did she mean she was lucky to be alive?

'I believe so,' she respectfully added.

'Right, step two. This is where I get directly involved in the case. I will send a series of emails to the police department alerting them to the situation, a tipoff, a snitch act, if you like. This will explain why Junge should be in his father's care.'

Sebastian cleared his throat, looked at Viola for a response to discern whether Tempest knew of the latest developments on the Ambassador.

'He's in a coma now, so does this still hold that Junge will be in his father's care?'

'He's alive is he not? So that will hold until we know otherwise. The boy is safe. I need Matthew Soto brought in within the next twenty-four hours.'

They heard a faint click, and she was gone.

Viola pondered whether the TT signature at the end of Tempest's messages stood for Team Tempest or Tempestuous Tempest.

Being on the wrong side of her temper was not pretty.

2 2

Sebastian bent over with his face buried deep in his hands. Never in his life had he been this humiliated. He made a point of never shaming his adult students. Being chastised his whole life for his height, his acne, and weight problems — he knew the pain of being made to feel different. What Tempest said made complete sense to him about being a team regardless of the situation. What made no sense was why she believed he had abandoned Viola. She exercised her right not to join him when he called out to her. He had to accept that he had broken Tempest's code of ethics, but he struggled to accept advice on where he erred — he hated a public shaming. He was close to Viola, but this situation with Tempest unraveled him because she believed he left Viola in harm's way.

'Look, Viola, I owe you an apology, I should have made sure you were safe before I left, but when you did not respond to my call, I assumed you opted to remain at the site. I knew that you did not want the boys to know that you were involved in this case. I am sorry. Neither of us expected the situation to turn out this way.'

Viola acknowledged that he called out to her to let her

know it was him fleeing from the site in the vehicle that brought Matthew Soto to the cottage.

'It's not your fault, I could not risk the boys knowing I was involved in the events that night. Both know me well, and that governed my decision not to join you.'

'I wish you had said that to Tempest, but what she expects makes perfect sense, team players do not leave each other without discussing outcomes and the possibility of changed decisions when dangerous situations might occur. I accept that I erred, please believe that I had every intention of taking you with me.'

'Let's forget this, I decided not to follow you, so please believe that. Now we have to dig deeper into this investigation so brainstorming our next move is our priority in locating Matthew Soto.'

Viola knew that Bernice's number had to be on her phone after she received her call a few days ago. Thinking through what she should say to Bernice without spooking her was necessary. She and Matthew were in a hostage situation some- where. Sebastian watched her puzzling through her thoughts, oblivious to his attempt to read her mind. Now she was her mother's daughter plotting her course of action. Her mother would be proud to see her prudent processing of information which she unsuccessfully urged Viola to engage in during her impulsive youth.

Viola had it mapped out. She ran her plan by Sebastian. He told her to record the call to Bernice which might be needed later down the investigative track.

The phone rang three times and an anxious male voice picked up the call, 'Hello,' Viola remained silent. The male voice repeated, 'Hello... who is this?' Then the line was dead.

'Bugger! That was the gunman,' she banged the side of her head, 'that must be him, he has Bernice's phone. Dear merciful

God, I hope he hasn't killed them.' She stared out the balcony door at the darkening evening sky.

'I doubt it, as I've said before, he is an amateur at this, edgy and unsure of himself, he must have them, unless there's some other threat or psychosis, I don't believe he would have killed them. We need to inform Tempest and pass on the telephone number for her to forward to her police contacts.'

'That's hoping he does not disconnect the number.'

'Yeah, true, but you now have a tracking link to where he is. What an idiot, answering a call from a private number!'

'He is working in a team. Somebody picked him up from the cottage.'

'Who knows, but my gut still says he is a lone operator.'

'This call can be traced to your apartment! But our phones are unregistered so we have some protection I suppose.'

Sebastian was unfazed by the suggestion that the call would be traced to his apartment. The boys would vouch that he was on their side as a protector in getting them away from a volatile situation to safety. Viola had to be cautious with her movements because of her Aurora connection.

TEMPEST WAS glad to have a number to track Matthew and swished off leaving Viola in mid-sentence when she asked to be advised when a location was identified, and whether it would implicate Sebastian.

'I will do this on my own if Tempest wants me to case the location where Bernice and Matthew are held.'

'Don't forget Bernice might remember you as the door-to-door salesman. Women rarely forget a nuisance!'

'It's still safer for me to be in the firing line.'

'Please don't say *firing line*. It gives me the shivers.'

While Sebastian waited for Tempest's feedback on

Matthew's and Bernice's whereabouts, Viola returned to Aurora Academy.

George was on duty at the gatehouse that night and waved her off indicating he would log her arrival time. She slipped into her little temporary home, glad to have some alone time. Her father's encouragement was, 'Artista be yourself no matter where you are, that is the only way to call any place home.' In her exchange teacher role, she accepted those words as the wisest she had ever received — in her vigilante role she had to wear many hats in the name of restoring justice and peace in the lives Tempest asked her to serve.

But her father's words carried her through the night of the accident that brought her driving to a grinding halt. She was driving to Melbourne for a friend's birthday celebration when across the Princes' Highway the woman ran out in front of her car. Both her legs and spine were damaged — she was wheelchair bound at twenty-three. Viola slipped into the darkest days of self-loathing and questioning whether she could have avoided injuring the woman. No amount of therapy had her driving again and that was over a decade ago. She ensured she never lost touch with the woman and visited her every week when she was in Australia.

Here at Aurora she had gained a few trusted friends, the silent smiling George, earthy eccentric Vince, and caring chatty Maria who mothered her in so many ways. Sebastian in his own endearing way, with his own insecurities was fast becoming her proclaimed little brother, the one she never had. Then there was Tempest entering her life at the time she most needed to feel worthwhile, that email that hunted her down and appealed to her sense of justice.

And so, she became the exchange teacher extraordinaire and justice seeker.

There were challenges juggling both roles, but she knew she could never go back to being one without the other.

Viola flopped onto the bed contemplating what her future would be like when her cell phone announced a message from Maria who wanted to know if all went well with her dentist visit. She apologized for letting herself into the cottage, and left some soft food in the fridge. Considerate Maria, as ever, had prepared a special meal. Angels existed contrary to her mother's view of the world through the many Shakespearean quotes that she hung onto, *Hell is empty, and all the devils are here.* Trust no one was her motto and led to Viola losing many a young sweetheart because of her mistrust. If only her mother could meet Maria, not only would she meet a live angel, but she would get a good lesson on how to be a caring mother. She never wanted her mother to be self-sacrificing, just to understand her and her needs.

She replied to Maria that she would see her tomorrow and ran a hot bath, her luxury after a day of many strange happenings.

VIOLA WOKE to a notification of a staff meeting before the teaching day. The meeting was to be held in the Olympus Seminar Room, a room she had not had the pleasure of seeing before. A quick message to Maria inviting her for a cup of tea later that afternoon made her feel better when she accepted.

Vince met her on the way down to the seminar room. It had to be an important meeting they both speculated if it was in the ornate Olympus Seminar Room. Vince was his buoyant self, dressed in a pale grey suit and bright pink shirt. He expected that Miles might have an important announcement, maybe he was leaving Aurora. His mock bow and closed palms salutation to her made her giggle and then laugh out loud when he said, 'Oh Divine Mother, where hast thou been? The darkness of your boudoir was a glaring fact. Mystery Mother is more like it! I came over to invite you to join me in my evening meditation.'

She couldn't resist the mirth of the moment, 'Hey Father Vince, sorry I had to go to the dentist and met a friend and so we supped.'

'Anyway, kindred spirit, I hope your old chompers have been repaired!'

'All good, thank you!'

'I hate these early mornings. They mess up my aura for the rest of the day. I prefer after school meetings if any at all.'

'Yeah, so do I. It was quite a scramble this morning with such a late notification.

THE OLYMPUS SEMINAR ROOM, already filled with staff, had Viola hurrying for a seat at the back. Much to Vince's relief only the back row was vacant. His loud sigh met with a few backward glances in his direction. He leaned close to Viola and whispered, 'I've offended the ministry. I should behave.'

At the podium under a bright ray of sunshine, emitted from the skylight, stood Jace Dimakos. Miles Alexakis was not in sight. Jace announced that Miles was down with a virus and would not be in for the rest of the week and next week. A few shuffling feet was a sign that minds were buzzing on what might have really happened to Miles. He droned on that staff should avoid the media. They were hunting for information on the Ambassador's situation. In that same breath he announced that there was a sudden resignation from a staff member because of family matters — it was always ill-health or family matters. Schools kept resignations private when there was something to hide, Viola noted. Jace then dropped in that they needed a replacement for Claudette and shut down that part of the discussion. She felt Vince nudge her and dared not look at him with Jace's fixed look on her. Why was he always searching her out at meetings? Did he have any suspicions or was it just the eyes of infatuation? Jace thanked the staff, and dismissed them, no questions asked or invited. Viola knew that if this was Blackwater Ridge Performing Arts Academy, there would be many questions asked on the head's whereabouts and the nature of the family problem Claudette faced. Rob Dwyer was often in a corner on such matters with him bemoaning to Viola that his job placed him in awkward situations where someone could be hurt by his decisions. Such was the nature of leadership. She promised herself that she would never pursue rank, upward mobility had the capacity to erode passion, and alter personalities.

THE REST of the day was uneventful until Maria dropped a careless word in Viola's ear. How she knew such personal details in a place that was a locked fortress was beyond her.

'That Ms Claudette, rude young woman, is pregnant and when she started to show they asked her to leave.'

'They can't do that to teachers or any worker.'

'Oh they can, they pay to keep the person quiet and off they waltz, free from responsibilities. Gossip in the kitchen is that she is carrying Mr Dimakos' child, hence the rapid exit.' Maria raised her eyebrows so high that Viola thought they would disappear under her hairline.

AND THE COMPLICATIONS on the school front mounted, adding another dimension that something was a little more rotten than Viola had initially perceived.

23

The next four hours were crucial to locating Matthew.

Tempest sourced his medical records — he was due for a medical procedure on his left leg in a few days. Should they wait for him to turn up and assume he was in hiding or should they push on and find him? Viola impressed that Matthew was a man that should not be judged before all facts were known. Her perception of his love and care for the child made him a good man.

Twenty-four hours and the clock ticked, waiting for no one...

Tempest's influence armed her with the knowledge that Matthew and possibly Bernice were being held in an apartment block in Patras, some a hundred and seventy kilometres out of Athens central. An Airbnb apartment was available in the block where the captives were held. Sebastian booked the apartment over the telephone. He was amazed at the ease with which he was able to do this — that he was legally in the country was all that mattered, just his air-ticket and no other source of identification was required. The snag was that he had to block book the apartment for the week. As much as he was still cringing from Tempest's telling off for abandoning Viola, he knew that she was the best boss he had ever had. Even though she stretched him, he sensed that she knew his strengths and pushed him to acknowledge and act on it just as she did with Viola, although with a little sensitivity to her needs. She provided all the background leg work and only expected the physical serving of justice to be expedited by her agents.

He picked up the keys upon arrival in Patras and strolled along the waterway. This picturesque city, the third largest, with Mount Panachaikon overlooking this cosmopolitan Ionian city allowed him to blend in — he wore a blonde wig and carried his guitar strapped across his shoulder. Patras was a city to twenty-thousand or more students, and this extra consideration was part of his need to feel included. The people of Patras were hospitable in welcoming foreigners. His strong American accent could win him a few friends.

The four-storey apartment did not offer a view of all apartments so being a tenant offered him greater access to what he needed to investigate.

Sebastian walked back to the apartment expecting the corridors to be bustling with students coming and going from classes, but it was strangely quiet. He changed into an overall, picked up his toolbox and snooped around the building as the maintenance person. He went down to the basement, opened his fold-up ladder and pretended to check the light bulbs and wall switches all the while praying that the building management did not make random checks. A little girl ran up to him to greet him when her mother let go of her hand to open the car door. The mother's fear when she saw Sebastian was obvious. She stiffened, marched towards her daughter and scolded her.

The streets were friendly. Closed spaces changed people's perceptions of each other.

'Did I not tell you *not* to speak to strangers,' she looked up at Sebastian on the ladder, 'sorry we're in a hurry,' she mumbled aware that he perceived her hostility.

Sebastian nodded, and continued to prod around the light fitting as he watched them leave.

An old man stepped out the elevator, he had a walker and stopped when he saw the ladder, plotting how to manoeuvre around it. He scowled at Sebastian.

'Is there a problem with the basement lighting? I didn't notice that there was, and the building management did not advise that a workman was going to be on site today.'

Sebastian felt the hairs on his legs and the back of his neck prickle, he had to be prepared for one of two scenarios — the building supervisor might throw him out and call the police or he could charm the old man out of his suspicion.

'Just a routine check, sir, nothing major, perhaps why residents were not notified. Here let me help you get around this ladder. I apologize for the inconvenience.' He hopped off the ladder and guided the man around it.

'Where's your car? I'll walk with you.'

'That won't be necessary, but awfully kind of you. Not much of that these days towards an old fella like me.'

'I insist, let me walk with you.'

'If it's not disturbing your work too much, that should be good. I'm off to see my physiotherapist this morning.'

Sebastian sighed with relief when the man drove off with a cheery wave. Close call. The movement in the basement stopped. He moved up to the fourth floor with a bucket and window wash to clean the glass next to the elevator. After fifteen minutes he heard a door close and footsteps approaching. He kept his head down, his cap pulled low onto his forehead. He whistled as he wiped the large glass panels and caught sight of the man's reflection.

He looked down at his bucket, dipped his squeegee into the sudsy water with his eyes still lowered. He saw the same shoes he saw a few nights ago through the slats from behind the doors of the moldy passage cupboard at the remote, abandoned building.

It was the gunman!

The gunman paid no attention to his presence, entered the elevator, and disappeared. Sebastian kept his eye on the elevator lights to be sure he had indeed left the building. Then he rushed down the corridor. If he heard the door shut at close range then the gunman must have come out of one of the first four apartments. He tapped on each door, one and two were dead silent, nobody was home. The third door left him with the distinct feeling that someone was in there.

He knocked

No response

He knocked again

Then he took a chance

'Matthew? Are you in there?'

A feeble woman's voice asked, 'Who's there?'

'A friend, I've come to get you out ASAP.'

'How can I believe you?' she hissed.

'I took Junge out that cottage the other night and his friend Big Ted left with me. They are in the safe care of police.'

He heard a deep sigh and pressed himself against the door.

'I don't have a key to open this door. He'll be back soon. Matthew is tied to a chair and locked in the bathroom.'

'You have to trust me on this. I will watch for his return and act on that. You must not say a word to him, is that clear?'

'Yes, please get us out of here!'

'I'll be back.'

Sebastian's toolbox had everything a handyman would need around a home and some medical supplies for emergencies. He was relieved when Bernice accepted that he was a friend, her only hope of being freed. The gunman was unperturbed by his presence on the corridor unlike the woman with the little girl and the elderly gentleman with the walker. This confirmed that the gunman was not a trained assassin. Sebastian's day was mapped. He camped outside the fourth-floor elevator. A full confrontational tackle was not possible if the man was armed.

An hour later, the elevator dinged, and the door opened, the gunman rushed out and turned the corner onto the corridor with such speed that he bumped himself against the wall. Sebastian walked down behind him with his bucket and toolbox. As he reached for his keys and opened the apartment door, Sebastian lunged at him, poking him in the thigh with a needle — he fell to the ground as the door swung open and landed an inch away from Bernice's feet.

She jumped away and peered at Sebastian with fear ridden eyes.

'Have you killed him?' Bernice asked covering her mouth.

'No, I sedated him, he cannot move for an hour while we clear out. Where's Matthew?'

'He's in the bathroom.'

Matthew was ashen, his wrists were purple with blood clots created by the tight ropes that strapped him to the chair. He looked at Sebastian with suspicion.

'Where is my nephew, Junge? Is he safe? Is he unhurt?'

'He was when I left him with the police, I have to get you both out of here, before this bag of lard moves again.'

'Are we free to go? Bernice asked in a quivering voice, close to tears.

'Yes, I will take you to the police station where I left Junge with Big Ted. You must not mention my involvement in getting you out of here, you must say you ran away.'

'But they will blame us for this man's current state.'

'It's a temporary state from the neuromuscular blocking agent I injected into him, it inhibits his movement, but not for long, so we better hurry, Bernice.'

'How do you know my name? Have we met before? He's gagging, it seems he can't breathe.'

'He won't die, don't worry. Let's get out, or he will kill you.' Sebastian released Matthew.

'I am going down to the basement to move the car to the street, come out through the front entrance and I will pick you up there and head back to Athens. Matthew run your hands in water, or better still dip them in this ice bucket but please hurry!'

Sebastian grabbed his belongings from his rented third floor apartment and hurried down to the car. He knew Bernice was puzzling over why he was familiar to her.

Then the dreaded deafening sound of police sirens! He had to get out quickly without Bernice and Matthew! Unlike him they were protected with the arrival of the police.

He waited in the car until the sirens stopped and drove out unnoticed from the basement parking. On the drive out of Patras towards Athens, he wondered how he would explain this situation to Tempest.

The sobering thought was that Matthew and Bernice were safe. He turned on the radio to listen to what went on in the world while he played handyman.

The announcement he didn't expect to hear hit him hard — the German Ambassador had died an hour ago.

24

Under watchful police guard, Bernice and Matthew were escorted back to Athens.

POLICE HELD the gunman in Patras and Sebastian returned to his apartment to hide out for a few days until he knew Soto's fate. He had no certainty on whether he could count on Bernice and Matthew not mentioning his involvement in the matter.

AT AURORA ACADEMY JACE DIMAKOS called another urgent staff meeting with an extended recess to accommodate the time needed to discuss pressing matters. Jace Dimakos favored holding his meetings in the Olympus Seminar Room. Viola speculated whether it was for the privacy of his agenda. This area of the school provided security away from students. A sneaky thought she dismissed was whether he was preparing himself for succession to the position. God forbid, that Miles chose not to return! A restless energy permeated the room.

Viola admired the teaching staff at Aurora who were passionate educators but in staff meetings they were strangely etherized.

Jace was fidgety, shifting papers that had nothing to do with his meeting.

'GOOD MORNING, all, I apologize for this sudden meeting. The German Ambassador has passed on, may his soul rest in peace. After a dawn meeting with Miles Alexakis, we decided that the school will close for three days, starting this afternoon. This is our mark of respect and solidarity with the Ambassador and the people of his country and our Prime Minister. Parents have been informed and will keep their children at home. The families keen to assist will host those boarders who are not leaving the campus. At this stage, until I have cleared it, they will remain in the boarding house. There are no duties stipulated for you except that you remain in Athens and be contactable. If I call any events or further meetings, I expect you to attend.'

He looked around the room with a hardness in his dark eyes as he scanned certain faces, finally focusing on Viola. Then he added, 'We collectively agree on media avoidance at all costs and no visits to the locations where journalists are camped — they are hungry for gossip, hence ruthless in what they will report. It is vital that they do not implicate us in this.' Viola thought it odd that the school's reputation was an issue with the Ambassador's death. Jace left much unsaid when he declared the meeting over. He punctuated his meeting with a good dose of 'I's' — he had assumed full control of the school with autocratic ease. This change perplexed Viola. Everyone walked out in a perfect line of silence with shoulders hunched and eyes downcast. What were they afraid of? How could they not want to know more? Whatever happened to the curiosity they instilled in their students?

Vince rushed to catch up with Viola, bursting to say something to someone he trusted.

'Hey, Ms Bardo, what is this? A school or parliament?' He bit down on his teeth in a snarl. Viola quickened her pace to deflect attention from Vince's irritation.

'Yes, I know, teaching takes second place to politics. Oh well, do as you're told after all we are only visiting teachers.'

Neither uttered another word on the walk back to their classrooms.

VIOLA'S MESSAGE to Sebastian confirmed that she could spend the next three days at his apartment. His one-word affirmative reply had her wondering what was eating him. She mulled over how students' parents received information before the staff were advised of the school closure.

Classroom attendance was low. Brendan Sanchez was away.

Could it be that he was still traumatized by the gunman's shooting, or was he advised by police and his father to stay home for a while? Tutoring was easy to secure when money was not an issue. Tutors were likely to lower their fees if the offer was to teach the PM's son. Even if it meant lowering their values, some would do anything to get inside the PM' s house. Human nature was fickle, but teaching was a blessing in raising a child's mind and lifting the spirit, yet pandering to the rich and famous was an increasing prevalence in society. While teachers were vital to the future of a society, they were at the bottom of the pecking order. Money and rank garnered respect. For Viola teaching and justice were synonymous. After having worked in a few disadvantaged communities, justice resonated with her.

* * *

As usual, Maria popped over to see Viola with a selection of butter biscuits she had baked for afternoon tea, even though most students were leaving the campus.

'Oh Maria, I will put on so much weight during my time here. I enjoy all your gustatory delights so I should not be complaining,' she laughed.

'You are always complaining about weight. A woman must celebrate her curves, which is why we differ from men — they are rulers, nothing special about that. See I know how to make puns too!' Maria chuckled then noticed Viola's open bag, 'I see, you are packing, going away for the three days off? I wish I could get away too.'

'I love your pun! Why can't you go away for a few days?' She could not let Maria know that she had to be fit and healthy, and for her it meant being lean if she was to carry out her investigations with no limitations on her energy.

'Some borders will still be around, and somebody has to feed them, and watch over them, I enjoy taking care of the students.'

'So, you will remain on the campus throughout the three days of closure?'

'Mr Dimakos has asked me to stay on, so what can I say?'

Viola studied Maria's lined face. While she saw a loving soul before her, there was something beneath the surface that spoke of a sadness she could not quite comprehend. Maria had a free nature, but on matters pertaining to her own world she could be strictly private. Had she more time to spend with Maria, she might get her to speak up to lighten some of the sadness that dwelled within her. The nature of Viola's work did not allow her to form close bonds over long periods of time while on teacher exchange, serving justice in the roles Tempest designed for her. Maria's stoicism guarded matters related to Aurora, although once she began unburdening her load there was no saying what gems she would reveal. This side of Maria's nature cautioned Viola not to reveal too much of her own life and moonlighting work.

'Will you pop in on the days that you are off, it would be nice to catch up for a cuppa when you are more relaxed without the demands of your teaching day.'

Viola saw a glimmer of hope twinkling in Maria's eye.

'Yes, for sure! I will be in touch and send you a text message to let you know which day I might come over.'

'I might have more news by then. Did you hear that the Ambassador's wife arrives from Germany tonight? She will have some tough decisions to make, so that will be interesting. I've said too much again, I should get back to the boarding house.'

'You know whatever you say to me, stays with me, so never fear on that score.'

'I know, I do trust you. You make sure you enjoy your days off, but let me know when you are coming in, and I'll bake you something special. Take care my dear.'

Viola watched her leave with drooping shoulders and an audible deep sigh. She felt the sting of Maria's loneliness.

WITH A BACKPACK CARRYING a few essentials she slipped out the school gate unnoticed as a relaxed mood settled around the closure announcement. George was not on duty that afternoon.

* * *

TODAY SEBASTIAN DID NOT MEET her outside the apartment. It was odd not to see his smiling, lost schoolboy face waiting for her to arrive. He buzzed her up to the apartment. He was unshaven, wearing a creased cotton shirt, and old gray sweatpants. The apartment was dark, the balcony door shut, and the blinds drawn.

'Hi, good to see you still in one piece. You did well in getting Matthew as Tempest wanted.'

'Not quite the way she expected. It could have failed; it was a close call. I don't know how the police got wind of what was happening at the apartment in Patras. But this tells me I should be careful how I move around this city.'

It startled her to observe how unsure he was, almost broken somehow.

'It's the age of surveillance and has been for a long time. No matter how careful we are, there is always that risk. Don't beat yourself up over that, we have to tie up some loose ends.'

He told her about the woman with the little girl, and the elderly gentleman with the walker. Both residents did not appear to think he was up to something sinister. Just a regular maintenance guy. He didn't think that they had reported anything to the building manager or to the police that he was a threat in the building.

Viola listened to what she saw for the first time as Sebastian's naïveté. He wanted to trust and be trusted, she understood that, and it was only those hurt by life who craved that acknowledgement. She also knew that he needed to redeem himself from the chastisement that Tempest leveled at him. That was a bitter pill for him to swallow.

'Have you called Tempest yet, or has she communicated with you since you got back from Patras?'

'Just a brief message, letting her know I was back. She is expecting us to call once we are together.'

Viola nodded and Sebastian dialed Tempest.

'Greetings dear agents!'

Her exuberance after the last conversation regarding the outcome of the stakeout, was a surprise.

'Hello, Tempest.' They both called out in unison.

'I am pleased that Matthew Soto is with the police, and Junge is safe, for now, under the Prime Minister's care, and happy to be with his friend, Big Ted.'

A faint smile danced across Sebastian's face. It meant a lot to have Tempest's positive opinion of him, yet she did not praise him for a job well done. Her whole leadership focus was on teamwork, team recognition, she never selected one over the other except in the last criticism of Sebastian's clear failure to ensure that Viola was safe. That was something that confused Viola. Her respect for Tempest was limitless, but this made her uneasy. Then Sebastian spoke, feeling himself again with Tempest.

'I still don't understand how the police got wind of this. Their timing was perfect, down to the minute.'

'Never fear when Tempest is near,' she laughed in her husky smoker's voice.

'Are you in Athens?' Viola exclaimed.

'Let's just say I have contacts in many places.'

With that last statement left hanging, she whisked off in her usual Tempest way.

25

Tempest's genial mood lifted Sebastian out of the quagmire of his despair.

For the first time, they relaxed since being assigned twelve days on the case. They spoke about their personal lives.

'We really know very little about each other, yet we have spent close to two weeks working together in tight situations.'

'Yes, work has consumed us, but I'm grateful that we clicked from the outset. I can't imagine what it would be like to work with someone on such matters and not get along.'

'Given the short time frame we had, had we not clicked as we did, the process would have been much slower, and we would have risked incurring Tempest's ill temper.'

'Ah, playing on the word tempest I see,' he reached across and playfully punched her arm, 'when I arrived in Greece for my sabbatical, I had no idea that I would take up a justice assignment. I don't know how or why Tempest recruited me as an agent. I must admit I have learned so much about myself.'

'Yes, working on human rights issues and social justice matters can be hugely beneficial in many ways.'

'So, what's the secret life of your curly locks, Ms Bardo?'

Viola enjoyed Sebastian's playful mood. He opened a bottle of bubbly and emptied a bag of nuts into a crystal bowl. He sat back in the armchair like a smug schoolboy waiting to hear a secret story. She felt a strange kinship to him and seeing him eagerly awaiting her life story softened her. Revealing the depths of her soul or her life past and present was not something Viola did easily.

From the minute he realized she was the daughter of an artist and literature professor, and that she grew up in different countries, and was of diverse demographic origins, he was filled with admiration and desperate to know more.

'You are an international citizen in so many ways — African, French, Portuguese, how exciting and an exchange teacher to boot! My background pales compared to yours perhaps I should stop and not say anything about myself. Wow, your father runs his own art gallery, what a wonderful life that must be!'

'Never compare your life to another that is the lesson my dear aunt Lorenza gave me. We are all unique individuals, products of our heritage and parentage. Now that surpasses professional boundaries and perceptions of affluence. So, let me tell you, my friend Sebastian, is a person I want to get to know better and I don't say that lightly.'

Sebastian's cheeks glowed, never in his life had anybody paid him such respect. He was ready to share the life behind his handsome face.

* * *

HE HAD deep-seated emotional baggage about being adopted although his aged American parents gave him a good life. They tried, but he always felt disconnected from them and their world. His antisocial tendencies kept him locked within the four walls of his suburban bedroom. He said that he had searched for his biological parents for many years, but each time hit a stone wall. His adoptive parents had no information on who his biological parents were. The only thing they knew was that he had a trust fund set up for him by his anonymous mother for all his educative needs. At eighteen she gave him ninety percent access to the trust fund with part of it frozen until he turned thirty. His biological mother left him a letter with the prerequisite that it be read once he had full control of the trust fund. Viola sensed his difficulty in controlling his emotions when he spoke of the letter.

'She wrote it in her own hand. The words are imprinted in my soul.'

> Forgive me I had no option but to place you in safe care far away from me. I pray every day that the situation improves so that I might reveal myself to you. You are forever in my heart. I remain your loving mother.

He paused, sighed, and continued in a softer voice.

'From the day I received that letter, particularly those lines, I have not been at rest. It left me more unsettled than I had been all those years before. My adoptive parents were upfront with me from the first day I could understand that I was not their biological child. I meant the world to them and I carried immense guilt that I gave half of myself as the son they loved and adored.'

He had the best in private education and received generous gifts every year for every birthday with no message attached. His stepmother assured him that the gifts were coming from his biological mother. She said without a doubt his mother loved him, but something had impeded her raising him. She told him his mother was a kind spirit and that he had the same in him.

His adoptive parents had since passed. He was alone and struggled to form lasting relationships, drifting from one thing to the next. The only steadfast aspect of his life was his university teaching which consumed the entirety of his life. His campus office was his second home. He worked late into the night, on constant call to support his students. During his formative years his parents lived a quiet life having no extended family themselves. Whether they kept away from family was something he was never told.

Viola interjected at that point, 'With due respect, Sebastian, please don't think me rude, I should be the last one to ask, but did you ever find love, someone that you wanted to spend the rest of your days with?'

Sebastian grew pensive and paused for almost five minutes.

'I did, but nobody wants to be with someone as intense as I am, someone who has no clear direction on where the relationship was going. I could not commit, and I do not blame the women I was temporarily with for walking away.'

Viola felt a tugging kinship with Sebastian. She had been there, never trusting that there would be permanence in her life. As a sensitive child who witnessed marital discord, she was afraid of commitment and the repercussions of an ill-fated marriage on the children of such a union. Her father told her that his marriage to her mother should not be a yardstick for her life choices.

'Well, that is the life that I have lived, married to my job and I will probably wind up dead in some city somewhere in the world where nobody will know me or even miss me.'

'That will not happen with me around. If you think you are rid of me after this assignment, think again!' She reached over and nudged him like a gentle kitten seeking acknowledgement.

'That's lovely of you, Viola, perhaps it's what I needed to hear. Let's face it, the lives we lead will scare any potential partner away. The secrets, the months away on assignment, calling from unknown numbers, really, who would want to be in such a relationship? If it happens, then thank God!'

AFTER MANY YEARS floating through her own life, Viola met a kindred spirit, fated by Tempest, who wanted nothing from her, someone she could work with and have a sensible chat with without judgment. While they were open with each other, she could never tell him the intimate details of her parents' divorce. She was fiercely loyal even though she suffered through those years. He would never tell her about the years of counseling he underwent and his suicide attempt. He said he received a timely email from Tempest while he was in Athens to assist on this investigation.

Work crept back into the conversation with Sebastian turning on the television to catch the latest on the shooting and death of the Ambassador. The part that grabbed their attention was the footage of the Ambassador's wife's arrival in Athens.

She was a statuesque woman with a wide-brimmed hat, so large it flopped about her shoulders, concealing a view of her face. Was this deliberate? Viola mulled over her secrecy. She held up her hands to deter journalists from getting close to her as cameras chased behind her stilettoed walk. A black sedan awaited her, and two suited bodyguards assisted her into the vehicle.

'I wonder if they will hold the funeral in Athens?' Sebastian asked.

'I wonder that too because his wife has arrived with such pomp and ceremony. But I daresay that they might fly his body back to Germany. As an Ambassador, the state decides his last rites, with limited input from family members.'

'It will be a while before those decisions come to fruition, although it all depends on what Germany wants.'

They spoke about Aurora and its history and governmental

association. Both believed the connection was because Miles was the Prime Minister's brother. Beyond that they had no clue to what created that unusual bond. Sebastian suggested that she draw Maria into a conversation on the relationship for clarity.

'It's the blue-collar staff who know more of what is happening both on the ground and in the upper echelons.'

'This is true, Maria has been there for a long time and I believe is privy to several insider secrets. I plan to go over tomorrow for a spot of afternoon tea with her, if she's still on site.'

'Good, that might yield more that we need. Without the bustle of a normal boarding house day, Maria might relax and be inclined to drop a secret or two.'

'She trusts me, I know that, but I would hate to exploit that.'

'We have to do what we have to do. What she does not know will not hurt her.'

With that settled, the conversation wafted to their dreams and passions outside education and serving justice. Viola was comfortable to talk about her poetry writing and that she intended publishing them someday. He dreamed of running a farm with horses and growing his own organic fresh produce and writing the stories locked inside him.

'What's holding us back? Twelve days is all Tempest gave us and look how far we've come,' Viola laughed.

He could not quite define why he wanted to serve justice but assumed it was due to his birth and subsequent life. She wanted to be a policewoman to solve the mystery of the disappearance of her beloved aunt Lorenza, but being a teacher claimed her as her aunt encouraged her as a child to pursue teaching to make a difference in the world. As much as she hated to admit it, her mother's job was also a draw card in her career choice.

Shared lives grew in closeness under an Athenian night, locked away in an apartment close to Syntagma Square.

THE NEXT MORNING Sebastian received the instruction to call Tempest as soon as possible.

The police in Athens received a letter written by the German Ambassador. It was mailed by his attorney in West Berlin.

26

———————

The Ambassador's letter to the police in Greece was shocking.

It convinced Sebastian and Viola that Tempest had an agent in the police force in Athens who kept her informed.

A well-planned handwritten letter authenticated by the Ambassador's signature made him the inarguable author. The revelation was calm and officious.

It is with great sadness that I pen these words upon the kidnapping of my beloved son Junge. Much will be spoken about me for I married in haste after the passing of his mother. My boy needed care that I could not provide alone, hence my current wife was sent to me as an arrangement for this need. At first, I did not make much of her aloofness. I put it down to her being a young woman in a new country, the age difference between us, and that she had a child, not her own, to care for.

That first year of mourning for my dead wife, I was oblivious to my new wife's behavior. Staff alerted me to her frequent departures to the city, on her own, leaving Junge in the company of a nanny that she employed without consulting me. All of this occurred during my trips abroad to attend to governmental matters. I let things remain as they were as the marriage was arranged and I had no jurisdiction over her heart or freedom. When the care of my son was jeopardized, I was compelled to address the matter with her. She denied that she was neglecting his care during my absence. There was not much else I could do. A week after my discussion with her I received an anonymous letter stating that I should watch my back if I valued my life. This was a direct threat which I lodged with my attorney. At that point we decided that we would watch and wait hence the matter was not reported to the police. Two weeks later Junge disappeared. Then another letter arrived. This was signed by Matthew Soto. Now, when I write this statement, I know it was not a letter written by Matthew. It was a forgery. The letter stated that he had my son and would kill me if I attempted to take the boy away from him. This reeked of a plan not well thought through. I knew Matthew for his astute military skills, and this confirmed that he had not engineered the letter. I have had no reason to believe that Matthew Soto, my brother-in-law, would harm my son. Junge loves his uncle dearly.

Today on this 11th day of November I declare without a doubt that if I am incapacitated by injury, disease, or die, I give full custody of my son, Junge, to Matthew Soto.

I am of sound body and mind in making this declaration which I have lodged with my attorney to fulfill when necessary.

Viola and Sebastian leaned back in their seats unable to respond to the declaration that Tempest read in an unemotional tone.

'What are your thoughts team?'

'I am pleased with the new arrangement for Junge's care, but we should probe into who the gunman is? What is his role in all of this?'

'Agreed.' Sebastian added, scratching his head, 'What a twist to what we set out to achieve. The Ambassador seemed to be an upstanding man.'

'I would hope so, Sebastian. He is… *was* my client.'

Sebastian kicked himself for speaking his thoughts. Did Tempest take offense?

'I am leaving you both to gather more information on the gunman and the late Ambassador's wife. I need everything you can dig up on her from her days as a student in Greece at Aurora Academy to the time when she left to become wife to the Ambassador.'

'Are you able to provide us with the details of the Ambassador's wife's whereabouts during her stay in Athens? I have a plan.' Viola was in command when she had an idea, and Tempest respected that display of initiative.

'Yes, I'll get that to you in an hour.' She whisked off.

'Is that listening device turned off?' Viola asked.

'No need to, the plot has thickened to bubbling point with two unknowns included to the initial investigation. Nothing is a secret so no discussions behind closed doors anymore. The dead man has left us with a strong connection to what the motive could have been. That is a massive lead that the police should pick up. We are merely the vessels in this quest for justice. I can't see what more we can add to the investigation apart from our observations and reactions to changed behavior from those that might be responsible for this situation. I just wish I could get out to poke around what else is going on with this case. I don't know if I can sit cooped up in this apartment for much longer.'

'Surely there is no threat to you now with the gunmen behind bars, right?'

'Don't bet on that, we don't know enough about him to assume that he was acting on his own. Remember, somebody picked him up after I left with the boys on that horrid night. I think he might want to put me out as I was a threat to his intention to kill the Ambassador.'

'Tempest would not allow that to happen.'

'How can you be so sure about that? I don't believe I have her respect.'

Viola explained that it was women's intuition — Tempest needed them and would not deliberately expose them to danger.

Sebastian was quick to question, 'And what about the night at that dreadful, abandoned building? Women never forget.'

'I beg to differ. You say that like some seasoned spurned Valentino.'

'Ouch coming from you that hurts.'

'Joking! Seriously we need to move on with a plan for how we will gather more information on the Ambassador's wife and the man behind bars. The latter might be a little more difficult.'

TEMPEST RETURNED to reveal that the Ambassador's wife was at a hotel in Syntagma Square. She provided the hotel name and room number.

Viola scheduled an afternoon tea with Maria at Aurora Academy and Sebastian went snooping around the hotel.

Poor Maria had to remain at Aurora because two lonely borders had parents who would not allow them to spend their days off with a friend's family. Teenage cousins with parents who did not consider the social lives of their children. They did not mingle socially and imposed the same on their daughters' lives.

'Are they politicians' children?'

'No, they are from business families in China.'

'I am sure they love being around you and I know how you must spoil them more now.'

'They are lovely girls just needing a bit of fun so I'm here to provide that and in some ways, they are company for me too.'

Viola was pleased to see Maria happier and relaxed. This was a cue to dig for whatever information she might have on the Ambassador and his wife.

'Anything interesting happening around the admin area while I've been away?'

'Nothing much except that there was a meeting this morning, a lot of legal eagles, suited and booted, a man, two women and Mr Alexakis was here. He looked rather pale, drawn, and gaunt. He must still be ill, I guess.'

'Was Jace Dimakos there?'

'Oh yes, he asked me to make a batch of scones for their morning tea. I didn't see them again as I was asked to leave the tea trolley at the door. I cleaned up two hours later after they left, on instruction from Mr Dimakos to do so.'

'Interesting, I would've loved to have been a fly on that wall. I wonder if it had anything to do with the Ambassador or just school related matters.'

'I don't know, and I don't think you should worry your head over those things, you will be out of here and I will remain to see more. Will you stay on till the end of the year?'

'I'm spending Christmas with my father in Porto, and not sure if I will stay on at Aurora?'

'I hope you do. It will be nice to have you around for a bit longer.'

They spoke about the lack of further information on the shooting of the Ambassador and Viola indicated that criminal cases were sometimes sensitive when political figures were involved, and the truth slept when the media was monitored.

'You understand many things not just your music. You must've done a lot of study in your day to know all the things you know. I hear the students speak about you at the dinner table or in the morning at breakfast, always saying, 'Ms Bardo, she's the best!''

'Thank you for that, Maria. They are lovely students. Once again it will be sad to say goodbye to them.'

WHEN MARIA ASKED what she was doing during her days off, she said she was helping a friend with a research paper, so she was still busy.

'Teachers never stop. Even during the school vacations if they are not away on a trip somewhere, they are always coming in, preparing, getting things organized for the new term, and clearing out old stuff. I don't know if this happens everywhere, but it happens at Aurora.'

'Being a *teacherholic* is a universal thing,' Viola laughed.

'Well, before you leave for Porto to see your father, I must have you over at my humble home for dinner.'

'Maria, I should take you out to dinner as you are constantly feeding me. Leave it to me I will arrange something before I leave.'

'Ah, you are too kind, but it would be nice to spend an evening chatting over dinner.'

'That's settled then!'

Viola knew that Sebastian would be unimpressed with the lack of details she had after seeing Maria. Vince was away at a midweek yoga retreat. The school was deserted without his colorful personality.

* * *

SEBASTIAN SPENT the afternoon waiting outside the hotel in Syntagma Square. He did not venture inside the hotel and sat outside on the bench near the drop-off and pick-up point at the hotel entrance. He had his laptop and was ready to work on his research paper. The watch and wait could take several hours. In unprofitable use of delay there was no success. At five minutes past two o'clock a black sedan pulled into the ten-minute pickup zone in front of where he sat. A uniformed driver got out the car and walked into the foyer of the hotel. Another ten minutes passed before he stepped out with a tall blonde woman in tow. She wore a loose floral dress that billowed around her on this windy afternoon. Her head was safely out of view under another large, ornate hat. The driver opened the backseat door for her and held out his hand to assist her into the car. At that precise moment a huge gust of wind blew in, pulling her billowing dress tightly across her midriff.

Sebastian observed with a keen eye, hidden behind his dark sunglasses, seeing what was unexpected — her pronounced pregnant belly!

27

Tempest's link to the police department in Athens was a necessary connection in a political investigation.

This confirmed they were working on the right side of the law for Junge's well-being — to Viola children were precious at any age and Sebastian valued family based on the limitations of his own childhood emotional struggles that bit deep in his teenage years.

The next lot of information needed was how and why Matthew removed the boy from his home without his brother-in-law's consent. They appeared to have an amicable relationship evident in the Ambassador's penning of his last wish for his son.

After extensive deliberation, Tempest suggested that Viola should meet Matthew Soto one more time to gain a closer understanding on his involvement in the kidnapping. Seeing and hearing the sting of emotions authenticated truth. In an age where fake news proliferated, a formal statement much like a press release or the evening news fed off sensationalism. Matthew trusted her, and she believed his intentions were noble in taking the child. She abhorred the word *kidnap* or *abduction* which did not fit her perception of Matthew Soto. The Ambassador's statement confirmed this.

By the twelfth day all parties, minus the Ambassador, were safe from harm, but the resolution had a few dangling pieces.

On Saturday morning Viola boarded a bus and arrived at Soto's front door unannounced.

Two police officers stood guard at the front gate. She explained that she was Soto's nephew's tutor, and that she wanted to know how the family was doing. The older officer called Matthew on his cell phone, and he allowed her entry into the house. She had to accept being frisk searched as she had entered an unresolved crime situation. Matthew Soto was not free of any involvement apart from the fact that he did not directly pull the trigger that killed the Ambassador.

Matthew looked thinner, dark circles around his eyes spoke of exhaustion.

'It's lovely to see you. You must be in shock just as we are after hearing everything the media reported.'

Bernice hovered at the end of the hallway, unsmiling, nervous, agitated. Both were shadows of their former selves.

Viola greeted her and walked towards her, she relaxed a little and invited her to take a seat in the lounge room.

'I apologize for turning up with little forewarning,' she explained that there was no way she could reach them apart from physically coming to the house.

'I'm glad you are both unharmed, how is Junge doing?'

'Don't apologize, it makes us happy that you came over. It tells us you believe we are innocent and care deeply for Junge's welfare.'

'A hundred percent! I saw the great care and love that you both gave the lad.'

Matthew's shoulders dropped as he drew a deep sigh of

appreciation. He explained that his nephew was under police protection at a safe location, but they were not allowed to see him. Telephone calls were permitted for a few minutes each day. The distressed boy wanted to return to his uncle.

'It has been too much for the little fella, now that his father is dead, and decisions are being made on his behalf.' Bernice's distress was her open wound in her secret life.

Viola's presence calmed them and soon a relaxed mood prevailed. This cleared the air for further questions on what had really transpired in little Junge's life.

Viola manipulated this atmosphere to unearth the truth behind the media hype.

'What prompted you take the boy out of Germany without letting the Ambassador know?'

Matthew gave her an unblinking gaze, pondering how to articulate what seemed so wrong, in an authentic, truthful explanation.

'I will have to answer that question many times over so I will tell you now, this is the truth I know, but, I will value your feedback on whether you think what I did was right or wrong. Will you do that for me, Ms. Bardo?'

For a second Viola felt that Matthew had imposed conditions on his telling of the truth. In her book the truth was simple, an unadorned truth — unconditionally the truth was the truth, regardless of how anybody reacted. She would accept nothing else but knew she had to play along if this was his game. She was an uncomfortable observer who was being coerced to accept his truth. Perhaps Matthew had faced too much recently that being blunt was his way to self-preservation.

She nodded.

He explained that he received an express mail package containing a DVD and a card.

The card's scribe urged that he get the boy out of Germany,

before it was too late. It was the DVD that pushed him to act as he did. The footage revealed the Ambassador's wife at breakfast, out shopping, and Junge's days with the nanny she appointed without her husband's permission.

The footage was disturbing. The nanny slapped Junge around the head and face, scolded, and locked him in his room, left him alone in the car when she should have taken him to the park or to his play group. During this time his stepmother was out either shopping, having her hair and nails done, or having coffee. Viola saw this as irresponsible parenting and a breech of duty of care by the nanny. How was this allowed to carry on without intervention by social services? Surely someone should have reported this to authorities. It occurred in public places. Carparks bustled with people going in and out of shopping malls and the general hub in social spots in cities, yet nobody said a word before this DVD arrived in Matthew's hands.

Viola was deeply disturbed with this horrific information. She heard Bernice sniff as rivulets of tears streamed down her cheeks.

'Seeing this footage killed me. It prepared me to do anything to get him out of this horrible situation. Junge was helpless while being mistreated and neglected as the Ambassador's son, how does that even happen? I believe my narration of the truth is accurate after seeing this footage in that the Ambassador kept mum to make his miserable wife happy.'

'Good God, the poor child must have been living in fear, in absolute hell.' Viola placed her hand on her heart, shaking her head at this inhumane treatment of a defenceless child.

Bernice stepped out the room for some air and returned with a pot of tea.

Seeing Matthew close to tears himself in revealing the trauma that his nephew underwent made Bernice teary again.

'Tell me, Ms Bardo, what would you have done had you been in my situation?' Please give me your honest answer.'

His pained words had no need for validation. He acted in good faith in wanting to protect his sister's beloved boy.

'To be honest, I would have called the authorities and handed the matter over to them. However, in saying this I don't understand the political power at play and whether that would have brought safety to the child. But you acted in the only way a loving uncle would behave or react after seeing such mistreatment. I don't think I will have the stomach to look at that after having met sweet Junge.'

Crimes involving children distressed and angered Viola. She continued, 'You should put all of this in an affidavit and send the DVD to the police department to ensure that the truth as you understand it, is revealed. Second to that, you must enlist an attorney as soon as possible. If so much went unnoticed, I believe that you are up against a larger force — it's your voice in the wilderness of a massive cover-up that has used a child to solve some adult issues.'

Matthew agreed and thanked her for her time and candid advice. She left concerned that Junge might need psychological intervention to heal from the abuse his stepmother had inflicted.

Being confined to the apartment left Sebastian with a hunger to be outdoors. They returned to his apartment after a slow stroll around the city centre. He was insistent that Matthew was a prime suspect in their investigation. A call to Tempest was necessary for another perspective.

'Hello again, team. Much has emerged in a few hours. She listened to all Viola had to say before she spoke. Her usual interruptions were absent.

'First... good on you for establishing a close rapport with Soto! This has allowed you to be privy to the truth not known by others here and abroad. We are sitting on information that we should expose to the right people for truth and justice to prevail.'

She explained that historically Matthew was not an easy man to converse with — sullen, obstinate, and rarely allowed women to lead the discussion or to offer him advice.

Viola's face and ears were hot. This was not the Matthew she had come to know. Tempest had more of an inside view on Matthew Soto than she had originally divulged.

Sebastian did his own due diligence that day. The black sedan picked up the Ambassador's wife and transported her to a rather palatial suburb on the North side of town. The driver escorted her to the entrance and handed her over to a woman in a white pants suit. He waited in the car.

Forty minutes later the door opened, and the Ambassador's wife stepped out, this time with a balding man in a black suit, white shirt, and black tie. He appeared to be between fifty-five or sixty years old. Olive skin suggested his Mediterranean background. His impeccable dressing and good looks gave the impression of a celebrity ready to walk the red carpet at the Oscars. Sebastian added that the Ambassador's wife looked a lot paler compared to when she stepped into this opulent home. She leaned back in the seat once the driver shut the door.

Tempest and Viola listened to the graphic details Sebastian provided. He included everything he could remember from the time, the disposition of the key players to the driver's reactions, and for good measure his own speculations on who the man in the black suit might have been. He had not done a background check on him. Tempest cautioned him to keep to the point and stop any talk that had no bearing on the case.

He revealed that the man in the black suit was a sought after gynaecologist serving the rich and the famous. A Dr Paean.

'He must be worth a fortune! You should have seen the home or consulting rooms or wherever he works, it sure is fabulous.'

'I'm sure he is worth a fortune,' Tempest said, 'but we have a dead Ambassador, his pregnant wife, and a driver in jail with Soto's fate hanging in the balance. In all of this there's an unhappy little boy who needs to feel loved, safe, and secure, and he's sitting in limbo. That by far is my priority.'

Sebastian listened without interrupting her and then piped in, 'We don't have the identity of the gunman — strange, don't you think?'

'Stranger than fiction!' Tempest laughed for the first time.

She cleared her throat and added, 'The plot thickens, dear agents, listen to this, are you ready?'

'Go ahead,' they both cried.

'I have it on good authority that the gunman confessed to a prison warden on his part in this whole sordid business. He declares that he kidnapped the Ambassador's son.'

'How? Is he in with Matthew Soto?' Sebastian's voice was shrill in his eagerness to know more.

'Steady there, Sebastian! One thing at a time!'

Before they could question her further, Tempest bid them a quick adieu and disappeared somewhere in cyberspace.

2 8

———

The history of the gunman was a mystery.

The media received an anonymous letter.

This made sensational news headlines. Everybody connected to the German Ambassador was on tenterhooks.

THE POLICE SUBJECTED all staff at Aurora Academy to security checks and random interviews. They called Vince in but by-passed Viola. Vince returned with his mood as blasé as ever. His criticism of politics was scathing. No politician he had ever encountered had any good to offer the people, they were narcissists exploiting the financial resources of the country leaving the people in need of antidepressants and psychotherapy. This was his general opinion regardless of the geographic location he inhabited.

Viola hunkered down, avoiding Vince to ensure that she did not draw negative attention to herself. In any other situation she would support his political views — not now with Junge's life unsettled.

The scandal seemed to make sense, the letter scribe knew

intimate details about an alleged love affair between the Ambassador's wife and the gunman. He was an ex-boyfriend who had returned to claim his prize. Together they lured Matthew into taking Junge out of the country to shift attention from themselves. The letter claimed that Mrs Ambassador was seven months pregnant with the gunman's child. He was a new employee as a bodyguard to the Ambassador. The detailed letter suggested that the deceased Ambassador had no idea that his wife was carrying a child that was not his. They had separate bedrooms until she came to him one night wanting to consummate their marriage, eight months after formalizing their marriage. A month later she announced her pregnancy. All the Ambassador wanted was for his son to be loved and having a sibling was the ideal solution to heal the void created by his wife's death. The gunman and Mrs Ambassador planned to have him killed, and the blame planted on Matthew Soto.

The nitty-gritty on how Junge arrived in Athens was explained as the workings of the influence and exploitation of power by a politician's spouse. She had the authority to allow the removal of the child without his father's co-signature.

This clarified why Soto escaped with Junge without detection for a safe entry into Athens. The Ambassador's wife had no restrictions imposed on her in her care of the boy. Soto had legitimate paperwork for accompanying a minor out of his home country.

The media spared no details in exposing the contents of the anonymous letter. Every person, on buses, trains, sitting at coffee shops and standing at street corners had their noses in the daily newspaper — reading and rereading, and debating how political wrangling had put an innocent child at risk.

Viola contemplated whether love or money was the motive for this horrendous crime.

Both were crimes of passion which sickeningly explained how a person could wantonly take the life of a person, after living with them for eight months with no indication of marital strife, except her hidden unhappiness at being coerced into the marriage. Viola believed that the Ambassador's wife hatched her intentions prior to the marriage and therefore had no claim to leniency on being coerced into her marriage. She thought of William Golding's, *Lord of the Flies*, and saw this situation as an inherent animal instinct where personal survival mattered above all else.

Viola stayed off the peanut brittle for two days. Now deprivation heightened her craving and restless energy consumed her. She had to stop the situation getting worse while a little boy waited for love and protection. They were on the brink of achieving this for him.

An awkward silence enveloped Aurora, Vince withdrew from sight to curb his careless tongue. His relationship with Viola was tense. He saw her as buying into the polluted political agenda at Aurora. If it had been any other situation, she would be shattered if misunderstandings sullied what her work involved. The child's welfare was her sole priority.

She immersed her role as a teacher with that of caregiver and protector of the youngsters in her charge. Apathy did not define her — she could never neglect reaching out to a weak, struggling, and vulnerable child. Vince was an adult who could deal with his disappointment in his own way. The altered mood at the school festered with the presence of plain-clothes police officers skulking in the shadows, listening into teachers' conversations, randomly popping into classrooms to observe lessons, and checking if there were agendas outside the school curriculum.

The media seemed to have no filter, or no filter was imposed now that dirty linen was out for public airing. A large center spread photograph of the Prime Minister's house revealed a home that was in lockdown. None of the occupants left and nobody entered the building. Brendan Sanchez disappeared from the school's radar after the night of the shooting. Nobody was asked to send work to him, nobody monitored or spoke of his absence.

Police officers lined the streets on either side of the PM's house, it was a fortress under twenty-four-seven surveillance. Viola was back under the terror the Frelimo wielded.

Was the Prime Minister now in danger or was there an international ring associated with the gunman? Why did he readily confess to a prison warden of all people? Thoughts tested her brain, heightening her need for a sweet crunch to deepen understanding.

* * *

As EXPECTED, a staff meeting was called after school. The Olympus Seminar Room was the venue once again.

Jace Dimakos stood at the front of the conference room, his ashen face and eyes fixed on the table. Once the shuffling died down, he looked up at Viola. His eyes darted back to the table. Those eyes tried to conceal the truth but never failed to find her.

'Sadly another tragedy has hit us today, hence the need for this emergency meeting. I will not go into the finer details of why we are here except to advise at all costs, again, that you avoid any media interactions on the situation. The Ambassador's wife is an ex-student of Aurora Academy and is deserving of our respect in not complicating the situation for her. Understandably we are in a state of shock that her name is linked with the gunman, but I believe that there is no truth in this matter. I urge you to be of the same mind to avoid any confrontation that might bring disrepute to our school community and those that have walked through these corridors.

I am appealing to you as dedicated staff of Aurora to support this decision by signing a declaration to the Prime

Minister's office that the school fully supports him and all our alma mater students. The school board has sanctioned this and I, as the messenger, carry this forward to you.'

Viola felt a sharp stabbing sensation in her chest, she had the urge to stand up, to say something, to uphold the truth as Matthew Soto revealed. Her tongue was thick, her pulse raced, but her lips froze.

She heard the sonorous wail of a steel chair dragged across the marble floor.

Vince rose to his feet not waiting for permission to speak.

'I have an objection to signing the declaration.' His booming voice, unlike the mellow voice Viola knew, drew horrified attention.

'What is your objection?'

'How can we assume that the Ambassador's wife is not guilty? That is a steep claim made without evidence that proves her innocence. Are you, as assistant head, saying that any student who has attended the academy is incapable of any wrongdoing? That is how I have understood what you have just outlined here.'

'Ah! As a foreigner, I do not expect you to understand how the Aurora family supports its own when falsely accused.'

'My *foreign-ness* has nothing to do to with my views. This is speculation not truth, right?'

Vince had no intention of letting things pass or stopping his line of questioning. A flushed Jace Dimakos' face glistened under the moisture that erupted on his brow and cheeks. He jumped to his feet leaving the gathering tense on what next to expect.

Some staff walked out of the meeting and Viola knew nobody had the power to stop Vince. He was on another plane, frustrated, and determined to have his say. She was not here to change the politics of Aurora. Just to teach and restore order in little Junge's life. Then leave.

The two people she counted on at Aurora, Maria and Vince left her shocked. She did not see this coming. Vince spoke up revealing his understanding of the truth, but he knew his tenure would soon end. Why did he rock the boat that might well end his teaching career?

AFTER THE MEETING Viola headed back to the cottage hoping she would not encounter Vince along the way. While it refreshed her that he had the courage to speak up, Jace Dimakos was right. He was a foreigner in these parts and therefore did not understand the code of conduct and behind-the-scenes expectations. Pandora's box was flung open, and the stakes were higher than the police presence at the campus gates.

She made a cup of coffee, curled in her lounge room armchair, and reached for a pen and paper and wrote:

> *Rumour or truth*
> *Fact or fiction*
> *Deception in diction*
> *Why is truth elusive?*
> *And the case inconclusive...*

SHE STARED at the incomprehensible words, ripped the page out, folded it and placed it in the pocket at the back of the book. She sat in the armchair until it grew dark.

Viola left Sebastian's message unanswered for two hours. He wanted to meet, and she knew it was not possible with the tight security outside the school. She had to let him know without saying too much. After a rethink she said it as it was.

Cyber invasion terrified her, but she hated lying to him. She told him it was best for her to remain on the campus, out of danger.

He picked up her message while scrolling through the internet and saw footage outside Aurora Academy — scores of police barricaded the entrance. It was a war zone gearing for an unknown attack.

Tempest called Sebastian, aware of Viola's lockdown.

'We need a little more patience before justice is ours.'

She spoke as one who lived between life and death, knowing that any outcome was possible.

Justice was not a mathematical delineation, human emotions governed situations, subjectivity was a challenge in their line of work.

As VIGILANTES of justice they operated under a lone sky.

That night unknown to Viola, Vince disappeared.

29

When Viola realized Vince left without saying goodbye, she called Sebastian to express her disappointment.

'I don't think he left. Although from what you tell me of his free nature that might have pushed him to do just that. But, with the way things panned out at your last staff meeting, the police presence and inside high-tech security and connections the school has, it does seems like he was pressurized.'

'In what way? To resign? Leave the country? Would they kill him?'

'I don't know, but they exerted some form of pressure for him to no longer be there.'

'I feel I'm living in the pages of a spy thriller. Nothing makes sense except that power controls and power decides. I'm not used to this.'

'Nothing new there, I'm afraid.'

'Why are you contrite about this?'

'To be honest, I don't mean to be, but there is nothing we can do about Vince's disappearance except hope that he will turn up like nothing happened, amused with all the fuss over his disappearance. So, stop stressing about that.'

'I am the only one making a fuss — nobody cares, so there won't be amusement from him when or if he returns! My life is one ongoing stress. You must feel it in our line of work. Teaching has its choices, and it comes with its own brand of stress. To put it plainly I don't do *no* stress.'

'I recommend we leave it there. Have you heard the latest on Junge's situation?' Sebastian would make a good husband to someone, he diffused situations with ease.

'No, what's happened?' Anxiety cranked up another notch, clear from her high-pitched out of character loud voice.

'I spoke to Tempest last night. Matthew Soto sent an affidavit to the courts on how he came to have Junge in his care. He might gain custody of the child given what his father revealed. Whether this will be a permanent arrangement is up in the air. Get this, the boy has been asking for Matthew and guess who else?'

Viola was unsure of what response he expected from her.

'The boy has been asking for you. You must have really had an impact on him because you were with him for just one day.'

'Do you know where Junge is now? Is he with Soto?'

'I'm awaiting word on that from Tempest. It seems the work here is over, don't you think?'

'Not for me, not until Junge is where he should be and is happy.'

Sebastian agreed that would be the ideal way to shut the case but either way they had to wait for word from Tempest. He asked if it was possible for her to come to his apartment after school for an undisturbed conversation with Tempest for their next directive. She agreed as police presence had dwindled outside Aurora.

Viola had two teaching periods after lunch and was annoyed to receive a text message from Jace Dimakos asking her to see him as soon as possible. She had three detailed reports to prepare for parents who had requested additional feedback on their children's performance in music class. When she thought about her colleagues in Blackwater Ridge Performing Arts School, she remembered the helicopter parents they referred to, forever at the school, wanting teachers to do more. Her mother told her to be quiet and do as her teachers required so there was no helicopter support from her teacher mother. Her father would write a scathing letter to the school on the mistreatment of his daughter. This was why she never complained about school issues to him. Her way around that was to be the best student a teacher could have. In an age where parents are consumed by their corporate lives, it was refreshing to see that proactive parents were not out to go to battle with the teacher or school but were seeking advice on how to help their children. This, Viola appreciated.

Now her time, fine tuning advice to parents, was disturbed by Dimakos! No warning like Rob Dwyer was mindful of... different strokes... so much had shocked her here at Aurora in her brief time. She should accept unpredictability. Her training as a teacher warned her about being flexible.

'HELLO, thank you, Ms Bardo for making yourself available for my late request.'

Viola was dubious about his sincerity. It made her wonder why he really wanted to see her, politeness was not always his way.

'I won't keep you long, I'm aware you are concerned with the sudden disappearance of the other exchange teacher.'

'Vince?' Irritation surfaced that he was dismissive in not referring to Vince by name, already making him a nonentity.

'No, I'm not.'

'That's good to know. What has happened around here has nothing to do with Aurora, but it has affected us. And, as we are human, these things can unsettle the general mood or invite thoughts of wanting to leave the school.'

Aha! This is what it was all about, him trying to figure out whether she would make a hasty departure. He had no tact, was transparent as a jellyfish and not in need of microscopic scrutiny!

She gave him a cold, challenging stare. He diverted his eyes looking at the heap of paper on his desk like he always did when he was cornered. The man was as predictable as a working traffic light! Jace blinked, tapped his desk while she waited for what else he was about to reveal. Perhaps he was one who might have been bullied as a child by parents or peers because one hard look from Viola made him meek. The cold stare was a passive aggressive ploy she detested, under *normal* circumstances. She had to test the mettle of a man who was pliable and sly. Dimakos in this moment was a baby whose milk had been snatched from him. After a few minutes of the awkward staring silence, he cleared his throat.

'I'm aware you have a few weeks left with us. This is the reason I called you in to ask if you would extend your contract until the end of the term.' After a fleeting look at her, he looked back at his desk waiting for her response.

'Thank you, that's very generous of you. Do you need an answer right away, or may I get back to you by tomorrow morning?'

'Tomorrow will be fine at least that gives me hope that you will consider it.'

She had to check on her Christmas plans with her father and whether he had scheduled anything for her prior to the festive period. Quality time with him was something she cherished, and she did not want to let him down at the last minute.

'Thank you, Ms Bardo, that will be all for today. I will see you tomorrow morning. Let my PA know what time you will come in, I will clear my schedule for you.'

The abrupt end to the meeting made her think that there was more that he wanted to say, yet he hesitated. She caught his pronounced reference to *my* PA and shuddered at what that implied for the future of the college. With Miles Alexakis she knew where she stood. His officious nature left no room for speculations. Rob Dwyer took her into his confidence, he was not an overt people person, his only weakness, but his administrative skills ensured he treated all with respect and he operated above the law. He sounded out decisions that were not confidential matters to gain a perspective on whether his decisions were reasonable. An understanding that women were more attuned to the intricacies of human sensitivities is what he respected. Why would she lengthen her time here with all that had gone down with Jace?

MARIA'S ABSENCE made Viola's days lonely without her cheery nurturing. She might be in danger, and with no telephone contact Viola felt she had deserted the one person who welcomed her with open arms from the first day she arrived at Aurora Academy. Her telephone line was disconnected, cutting off before she could complete the number.

She welcomed being with Sebastian that afternoon to elevate her need to feel she was an older sister, but respected him as a wise little brother. It surprised her how soon she had grown close to him.

They turned on the television channel for an update on the deceased Ambassador. A tribute kicked off highlighting his background — his father was German, but his mother was Greek which was no surprise given his connection with the Prime Minister and his shared sensitivities with the people of Athens. And he was a human rights activist and an advocate for climate change. He was a philanthropic champion of the poor providing shelter for the homeless in high-rise apartments in Berlin which he financed from fundraising drives and his personal funds.

The announcement at the end of the feature caught them off guard, the Ambassador's body was being flown back to Berlin the next day for a state funeral at the end of the week. It saddened Viola that she knew the calibre of the man, after his death. So many people were unknown in the living years for the virtues they possessed, death gave some the dignity life denied. Matthew Soto's affidavit was given a mention as corroborating the deceased's perception of who he was in relation to his son. The release of the boy to Soto would only happen after extensive psychological testing of Matthew and verification after extended observation that the boy enjoyed being in his care.

'Now that is a huge weight lifted from my shoulders. It's good to know that Junge will be in Matthew's custody.'

'Your intuition was on the money. Perhaps I should take great heed.' Sebastian winked.

They thought it was fair for the Ambassador's wife to remain under house arrest until the birth of her baby and thereafter she would serve a prison sentence although the state had not set the timeframe.

A life sentence was imposed upon her lover.

She lost everything — high social standing in Athens – friends, alienation from the people of Germany, and in time to come who knows what her unborn child would think of her. That would be her life sentence.

'In my eyes we have achieved justice.'

'So, what do you plan to do now? When do you head back to Australia?'

'Interesting that you should ask. Dimakos called me in before I left this afternoon and asked me to consider staying on till the end of the term. I might after I check in with my father to ensure that I don't clash with any of his plans.'

'That's good! Your vigilante role is unknown hence he wants you to extend your contract. I will be here for another two weeks before I return to New York.'

'We had twelve days to achieve our outcome, so I daresay we have been a good team.'

For the second time since she met Sebastian, she saw him as a little boy for whom praise was the best accolade he received. She felt a twinge of sadness for him knowing that she had unconditional love and unremitting praise from her father. What did Sebastian have? He said he thought his parents loved him. He knew it but did not know how to feel that love.

'Once Tempest gives us the sign-off, we can take in some of the sites of common interest. The only thing connected to a little bit of sightseeing was when we went to the changing of the guard and then onto the markets. The day we were saw Matthew Soto, the woman we now know as Bernice, and Junge. So much has happened after that.'

'This business changes by the minute,' Sebastian laughed, 'if only we knew then what we know now! Such is the nature of a vigilante's work. It takes the patience of a Buddhist monk to enjoy all of this.'

'For sure, and the same can be said of life. That is why I need my peanut brittle. You should take up the habit too,' she teased.

'Not after Dr Horatio telling you to toss the habit.'

They teased each other without caution, no longer sensitive to what they construed as one judging the other. It perhaps takes two people working so closely together with their lives at risk that brings a sense of trust and comfort when one knows the other has their back.

Lost in the moment, seduced into a comfortable mood they were oblivious to the beeping announcement that Tempest was on the line. Sebastian grabbed the phone when he finally heard it.

'Hello team! You took your good old sweet time picking up my call. Hey, it's not over until the fat lady sings.'

Silence.

'What's up team? Lost your sense of humor?'

Now they had permission to laugh.

Sebastian explained that they had watched the special broadcast on the Ambassador's life and that he had recorded it for her.

'Not necessary, Sebastian, I've seen it already hence my call. Don't forget I'm the queen of the airwaves! Nothing evades me.'

Viola heard the authoritarian voice Tempest adopted when she spoke to Sebastian – drilling into him that she was the boss lady. With Viola she was the voice of caution taking a more sensitive approach with her.

'I have one more request of you, Viola, before I close shop on this case. The Ambassador, our client, requested we ensure that his son was not only safe but also happy. He wanted his son to have a say on where he wanted to live.'

'What do you propose I do?'

'What do you think I propose?' There was the instructor's voice, this time directed at Viola.

'Pay Matthew Soto a visit to get a clear sense of whether the child is as his father requested. I know he will be, given what you have said in your earlier observations regarding Matthew Soto. That is all for today folks.'

Tempest switched off.

30

The embers had not settled. Viola had to visit Soto's home.

Was this to be her final step in bringing closure for little Junge? There were so many children in the world in need of love and care, but this little lad crept in and remained in her heart.

On Saturday morning she called Bernice who was ecstatic to have Junge back with her and Matthew. It did not matter that this might be a temporary arrangement, but to have the boy with them meant the world to her.

Joy filled their home. Matthew's aura was bright.

There was no sign of Junge. The train set Matthew had purchased for Christmas held his fascination. The only boy in the world to receive his gift before the celebratory day. She spent an hour and a half at the house to confirm what she already knew. The lad had everything he needed, a caring doting Bernice showered him with maternal affection, and Matthew was an ideal male role model.

Matthew's question caught Viola off guard.

'Would you consider joining us again to assist with the boy's care. His English has improved although I think he would gain far more with your ongoing tutoring.'

She paused a while contemplating whether she should take on two days a week with Junge and then realized that would confuse him when she departed for Porto in a few weeks. There was nothing worse than a child feeling abandoned. Lord knows she knew it. Lorenza left without a word. Matthew's hesitation in asking her to consider the position made her uncomfortable.

She had to think without emotions for what would be best for the child. While her heart was with him, she could offer nothing long term.

'I wish I could take up the offer, however, I'm heading to Porto. I would rather not commit to a temporary position that might unsettle Junge, if I left too soon. Children form attachments that could prove problematic. I'd scar him for life with thinking that people are ships passing in and out of his life.'

Matthew nodded looking into her eyes, trying to understand the woman behind them.

'Well, he might not be the only one.' This telling yet elusive response set her heart racing.

Bernice had to have been listening at the door to walk in on that awkward moment of silence between them.

'You two should go out to dinner, I will watch over Junge, there are no threats to his safety now, so go out.'

Her choice of *you two,* created a sense of familiarity, as though it was an expectation that she would accept the offer. Viola hated feeling ensnared, and, she was quick to respond.

'I would love that but...,' she caught the injured look in Matthew's eyes. All they had, was an officious formal meeting. Nothing more, why should she feel beholden to him?

She continued, 'I have arrangements for tonight and must pack for my trip to Porto.'

'Any other day?' Matthew asked, as Bernice edged her way out of the room.

'I can't be definite about that right now. I will keep you posted if I there is an opportunity to catch up with you again.'

'If I don't hear from you, trust me I will call you.'

Viola did not react to the comment. On one hand it felt like a threat. Then she accepted with a semblance of reluctance that perhaps it was endearing. Either way she was uncomfortable with how the afternoon was unfolding. For the first time she saw the crinkling corners of Matthew's eyes and the faint teasing smile lingering on his lips. Up to this point he had been stressed that he had brought the boy to Athens without his father's consent.

She forced herself to say, 'That's good,' without sounding nervous, 'I must go now, it was lovely seeing you again. Junge has been busy with the train set he loves so much. Good luck with everything! It is pleasing to see that the lad is so well settled. This is his home.' She extended her hand and hoped he did not notice how flushed and awkward she was.

He walked towards her, his eyes intense and unsmiling now, he bent down and kissed her on the cheek.

'Thank you so much for saying that, for being here when we needed you.'

A shiver riveted through her. She had only spent one day in the house with the boy and Bernice. What difference could she have made in just a day? Or did he know more about her?

Viola walked into the dining room to say goodbye to Junge. He looked up at her, and jumped to his feet.

'Don't go, don't go, stay, please play, Viola-Viola!'

He held both her legs like he did that first day she spent with him. Matthew untangled his arms and lifted him up.

'Well, that's two of us.'

She was ready to run. Matthew had turned weird on her

and she did not know how to react to someone who was still very much a stranger.

'Ms Bardo will be back to see us again soon, won't you, Ms Bardo?'

His wistful stare was hard to avoid. It forced her to agree that she would try to come back again soon.

She left the house feeling compelled to return. Today she could hop and skip her way to meet Sebastian without a care in the world.

SEBASTIAN MET her at the fountain in Syntagma Square. It was a warm day and unlike him, Viola found the heat unbearable.

'Did everything go well with Matthew Soto? Is the boy happy?'

'Yes, I'll explain in a moment, but can we please get out to a cooler spot — it's too hot here today.'

'Hey, African Australian girl! You should be used to the heat.'

'I'm not, American boy! You have hot weather in your country too and don't forget I'm part French and Portuguese. European lest you forget.'

'Oops sorry Ms United Nations! Let me get you to a cooler spot.'

'Good idea because I am known for my ferociousness in extreme heat. And trust me you don't want to be around me when that happens,' she laughed. Somehow with Sebastian there were no pretenses, she was Viola with no facades or the need to impress.

They headed to a gelato parlor which was a stone's throw away from Syntagma Square, and like two happy kids they licked on their pistachio ice-cream.

'Things went well with Matthew Soto, and the reason for

my visit has delivered as I had always expected. The boy is happy and loved.'

'Anything else?'

'Nothing else, why do you ask?'

'I feel you are withholding something. You seem eager to shut that door. Are you a hundred percent sure that everything is well with the boy?'

She cringed. How could Sebastian know her this well? Had she become transparent since she arrived in Athens? She knew she had to tell him about Matthew's strange behavior.

'Matthew asked me if I would consider coming back to work for him as an English tutor to the boy. I declined, but he seemed insistent.'

'So, did you yield?'

'No, I didn't. But I might keep in touch with Matthew just to know how little Junge is doing. Matthew is an all-round good guy, you know.'

Sebastian threw her a furtive sidelong glance. She seemed mellow and dewy-eyed after this visit.

'Lucky you! You will have a job any time you return to Athens.'

Viola was subdued thereafter, and Sebastian suggested a visit to the art gallery was what they needed to be in a cooler place.

She followed him around like a puppy preoccupied with the events of her afternoon. The gallery made her nostalgic wanting to be with her father, unsure of whether she did the right thing in agreeing to stay on at Aurora until the end of the term. Her father had an artists' in-residence week right until the week before Christmas which meant she would be on her own while he was busy.

. . .

Lost in this maze, she was aware of a familiar figure on the left side of the gallery.

The man dressed in a white suit was in conversation with an art dealer. When he turned to the side, she saw his profile. It was the dentist, Dr Horatio.

'Sebastian,' she hissed, 'let's walk the opposite way, that's my dentist on the other side, talking to the art dealer.'

'I reckon we should go up to him, your elusive Dr Horatio might have a few nuggets of information to share with us.'

'The case is closed,' she whispered, 'let's get out of here before he sees us, or else we will be here all night until the gallery closes. He doesn't shut up. How will I explain who you are?'

'Oh stop it! You can say I am your brother.'

Sebastian grabbed her arm and pulled her toward Dr Horatio. Soon she was standing in his line of vision. He spotted her and advanced in her direction like a lion ready to pounce on prime prey.

'Ms Bardo! Fancy running into you here!'

'Oh! Dr Horatio, likewise.' She struggled to muster the enthusiasm he displayed.

Sebastian stood close behind her, wagging his tail in puppy eagerness, waiting for an introduction.

'Who do we have here with you today?' Dr Horatio's condescending tone annoyed her.

'This is my friend...' before she could finish, Sebastian cut in.

'I'm her brother.'

Dr Horatio ignored Sebastian and turned to Viola.

'You didn't mention you had family in Athens.' His voice was an accusation, not casual curiosity.

'He has just arrived from America.'

'I see.' He changed the topic, 'Terrible the way things

turned out with the Ambassador's case, didn't it? Who would've thought his wife was such a harlot!'

Viola was silent, and Sebastian was wired to hear more from Dr Horatio.

Men! Viola did not want to discuss the situation with her dentist.

She thanked all her ancestors and angels in the heavens when she heard a husky female voice behind her.

'Steve! Steve Horatio! How many years has it been?'

Viola stepped aside to let the husky voice position herself in front of Dr Steve Horatio.

She tugged at Sebastian's arm to sidle away from this diversion.

'Lorna! Darling! Lovely to see you! It has been a long time. Heard about your divorce.' Dr Horatio bellowed.

'Phew! That was lucky! Just in time too!'

'Look at you, it's like you won the lottery. He must be an insufferable man if you are reacting this way.'

'Did you not hear him? I tried to warn you,' she laughed.

* * *

TEMPEST CALLED for a final wrap up.

She was overjoyed that Junge was settled in the Soto household.

'All the boxes are checked, well done team!'

They chimed in thanking her for her support, guidance and valuable information that helped with the investigation.

'You both should take a holiday now. Get to know each other on a social level. Who knows I might team you up again on another case someday?'

Sebastian gushed that it would thrill him to work with Viola again. She kept shut, unsure of whether she could trust him again after the stunt he pulled with Dr Horatio.

'Enjoy yourselves, angels!'

She whisked off with her usual grace.

'Did I hear that correctly,' Sebastian asked, a deep frown creased his brow, 'did she say *angels* instead of agents?'

'A little slip. I don't think it was intentional.'

Sebastian did not believe it was a slip.

Tempest was thorough in all she did.

* * *

THEY SPENT the days they had left together touring around Athens, stopping at too many ice-cream parlors.

When Sebastian left for New York, Viola counted the days to her arrival in Porto.

She did not encounter Vince nor Maria at Aurora Arts Academy in her final weeks there.

The flight to Porto was a welcome departure after twelve gruelling days, followed by fun-filled days with Sebastian and two weeks of loneliness. She rejected Soto's calls and was not sure if she would return to Athens soon.

All she wanted now was to hear the caramel tones of her father's voice when he said, 'Artista, you have arrived!'

The End

Is it a world to hide virtues in?

~William Shakespeare's Twelfth Night~

AFTERWORD

My passion for teaching and writing are closely aligned hence I thought I would share my perceptions on the role of teachers and why I had this vision of Viola Bardo as teacher and justice seeker.

Teaching is never singular in the manifold duties as educator, nurturer, social justice initiator, carer, and person that a child/student/peer can trust. In my growing up years I have been blessed to have had teachers who opened my ears and eyes beyond the confines of a narrow-minded apartheid system. Equally my parents ensured that apartheid did not define the course of my life. It is as a consequence of my visionary mentors, the wonderful schools I attended, and the friendships forged that I uphold :

In our angst and joy we are ONE under the sky of humanity.

Within perceived or self-labeled imperfection lies a wealth of perfection. Teachers celebrate and grow this wealth in their students.

Fundamental to the role of a teacher is respect for all. This in turn generates self-respect and cradles students to exude the same.

All Lives Matter is drawn into my stories from this foundation of my teaching and childhood experience growing up in apartheid South Africa.

Relationships are core to leadership and every teacher, every upholder of peace and justice regardless of the occupation they inhabit is a significant cog to a safe and secure society.

The fictional character, Viola Bardo, emulates the multifaceted duties of a teacher with music in her blood and the capacity to selflessly serve others.

DID YOU ENJOY THE FIRST BOOK IN THE BARDO TRILOGY?

If you've enjoyed reading, *Aurora Days - (The Bardo Trilogy 1)* please leave an honest review on your chosen platform to help other readers decide if they might like to read my books. This will help me to write more.

WITH GRATITUDE,

Mala Naidoo
www.malanaidoo.com

D o you enjoy trilogies?
Have you read the *Souls Collection,* an eBook box-set
and print editions that can be read as standalone novels or as a
trilogy? A mother and her daughters leave South Africa for
Australia but will their secrets follow them? Meet Grace and
Patience, a doctor and social worker, as sisters from different
cultural backgrounds.

www.ingramcontent.com/pod-product-compliance
Lightning Source LLC
Chambersburg PA
CBHW020137120726
47903CB00007B/2300